HATE MATE

A SOMERSET HARBOR NOVEL

CARGILL BROTHERS
BOOK 1

CHARLOTTE BYRD

RONAN BYRD

BYRD BOOKS

Proofreaders:

Renee Waring, Guardian Proofreading Services, https://www.facebook.com/GuardianProofreadingServices

Visit my website at www.charlotte-byrd.com

 Created with Vellum

PRAISE FOR CHARLOTTE BYRD

"Twisted, gripping story full of heat, tension and action. Once again we are caught up in this phenomenal , dark passionate love story that is full of mystery, secrets, suspense and intrigue that continues to keep you on edge!" (Goodreads) ☆☆☆☆☆

"Must read!" (Goodreads) ☆☆☆☆☆

"Charlotte will keep you in suspense!" (Goodreads) ☆☆☆☆☆

"Twisted love story full of power and control!" (Goodreads) ☆☆☆☆☆

"Just WOW...no one can weave a story quite like Charlotte. This series has me enthralled, with such great story lines and characters." (Goodreads) ☆☆☆☆☆

"Charlotte Byrd is one of the best authors I have had the pleasure of reading, she spins her storylines around believable characters, and keeps you on the edge of your seat. Five star rating does not do this book/series justice." (Goodreads) ☆☆☆☆☆

"Suspenseful romance!" (Goodreads) ☆☆☆☆☆

"Amazing. Scintillating. Drama times 10. Love and heartbreak. They say what you don't know can't hurt you, but that's not true in this book." (Goodreads) ☆☆☆☆☆

"I loved this book, it is fast paced on the crime plot, and super-hot on the drama, I would say the perfect mix. This suspense will have your heart racing and your blood pumping. I am happy to recommend this thrilling and exciting book, that I just could not stop reading once I started. This story will keep you glued to the pages and you will find yourself cheering this couple on to finding their happiness. This book is filled with energy, intensity and heat. I loved this book so much. It was super easy to get swept up into and once there, I was very happy to stay." (*Goodreads*) ☆☆☆☆☆

"BEST AUTHOR YET! Charlotte has done it again! There is a reason she is an amazing author and she continues to prove it! I was definitely not disappointed in this series!!" (*Goodreads*) ☆☆☆☆☆

"LOVE!!! I loved this book and the whole series!!! I just wish it didn't have to end. I am definitely a fan for life!!! (*Goodreads*)

"Extremely captivating, sexy, steamy, intriguing, and intense!" (*Goodreads*)

"Addictive and impossible to put down." (*Goodreads*)

"What a magnificent story from the 1st book through book 6 it never slowed down always surprising the reader in one way or the other. Nicholas and Olive's paths crossed in a most unorthodox way and that's how their story begins it's exhilarating with that nail biting suspense that keeps you riding on the edge the whole series. You'll love it!" (*Goodreads*)

"What is Love Worth. This is a great epic ending to this series. Nicholas and Olive have a deep connection and the mystery surrounding the deaths of the people he is accused of murdering is to be read. Olive is one strong woman with deep convictions. The twists, angst, confusion is all put together to make this worthwhile read." (*Goodreads*)

"Fast-paced romantic suspense filled with twists and turns, danger, betrayal, and so much more." (*Goodreads*)

"Decadent, delicious, & dangerously addictive!" (*Goodreads*)

"Titillation so masterfully woven, no reader can resist its pull. A MUST-BUY!" (*Goodreads*)

"Captivating!" (*Goodreads*)

"Sexy, secretive, pulsating chemistry…" (*Goodreads*)

"Charlotte Byrd is a brilliant writer. I've read loads and I've laughed and cried. She writes a balanced book with brilliant characters. Well done!" (*Goodreads*)

"Hot, steamy, and a great storyline." (*Goodreads*)

"My oh my....Charlotte has made me a fan for life." (*Goodreads*)

"Wow. Just wow. Charlotte Byrd leaves me speechless and humble… It definitely kept me on the edge of my seat. Once you pick it up, you won't put it down." (*Goodreads*) ☆☆☆☆☆

" Intrigue, lust, and great characters...what more could you ask for?!" (*Goodreads*) ☆☆☆☆☆

WANT TO BE THE FIRST TO KNOW ABOUT MY UPCOMING SALES, NEW RELEASES AND EXCLUSIVE GIVEAWAYS?

Sign up for my newsletter and get a FREE book: https://dl.bookfunnel.com/gp3o8yvmxd

Join my Facebook Group: https://www.facebook.com/groups/276340079439433/

Bonus Points: Follow me on BookBub and Goodreads!

ABOUT CHARLOTTE BYRD

Charlotte Byrd is the bestselling author of romantic suspense novels. She has sold over 1.5 Million books and has been translated into five languages.

She lives near Palm Springs, California with her husband, son, a toy Australian Shepherd and a Ragdoll cat. Charlotte is addicted to books and Netflix and she loves hot weather and crystal blue water.

Write her here:

charlotte@charlotte-byrd.com

Check out her books here:

www.charlotte-byrd.com

Connect with her here:

www.tiktok.com/charlottebyrdbooks

www.facebook.com/charlottebyrdbooks

www.instagram.com/charlottebyrdbooks

Sign up for my newsletter: https://www.subscribepage.com/byrdVIPList

Join my Facebook Group: https://www.facebook.com/groups/276340079439433/

Bonus Points: Follow me on BookBub and Goodreads!

- amazon.com/Charlotte-Byrd/e/B013MN45Q6
- facebook.com/charlottebyrdbooks
- tiktok.com/charlottebyrdbooks
- bookbub.com/profile/charlotte-byrd
- instagram.com/charlottebyrdbooks
- twitter.com/byrdauthor

ALSO BY CHARLOTTE BYRD

All books are available at ALL major retailers! If you can't find it, please email me at charlotte@charlotte-byrd.com

Somerset Harbor

Hate Mate (Cargill Brothers 1)

Best Laid Plans (Cargill Brothers 2)

Picture Perfect (Cargill Brothers 3)

Always Never (Cargill Brothers 4)

Tell me Series

Tell Me to Stop

Tell Me to Go

Tell Me to Stay

Tell Me to Run

Tell Me to Fight

Tell Me to Lie

Tell Me to Stop Box Set Books 1-6

Black Series

Black Edge

Black Rules

Black Bounds

Black Contract

Black Limit

Black Edge Box Set Books 1-5

Dark Intentions Series

Dark Intentions

Dark Redemption

Dark Sins

Dark Temptations

Dark Inheritance

Dark Intentions Box Set Books 1-5

Tangled Series

Tangled up in Ice

Tangled up in Pain

Tangled up in Lace

Tangled up in Hate

Tangled up in Love

Tangled up in Ice Box Set Books 1-5

The Perfect Stranger Series

The Perfect Stranger

The Perfect Cover

The Perfect Lie

The Perfect Life

The Perfect Getaway

The Perfect Stranger Box Set Books 1-5

Wedlocked Trilogy

Dangerous Engagement

Lethal Wedding

Fatal Wedding

Dangerous Engagement Box Set Books 1-3

Lavish Trilogy

Lavish Lies

Lavish Betrayal

Lavish Obsession

Lavish Lies Box Set Books 1-3

All the Lies Series

All the Lies

All the Secrets

All the Doubts

All the Lies Box Set Books 1-3

Not into you Duet

Not into you

Still not into you

Standalone Novels

Dressing Mr. Dalton

Debt

Offer

Unknown

ABOUT HATE MATE

Get ready for a sizzling enemies-to-lovers romance in Hate Mate by USA Today bestselling author Charlotte Byrd and Ronan Byrd!

Meet Sawyer Cargill, a bad boy billionaire CEO who has everything - except for a good reputation. After a video of him trashing the locals goes viral, he needs a PR fixer to save his family's business, the Somerset Yacht Club.

Enter Willow Anderson, a successful PR fixer who has a score to settle with Sawyer. **As his former high school bully victim, she agrees to take on his case for one reason: revenge.** But as she works closely with Sawyer, old feelings start to resurface, and she finds herself falling for him.

Can she forgive Sawyer for his past sins, or will their history be too much to overcome? And with the yacht club's expansion plans in jeopardy, Sawyer will need all the help he can get to save his family's legacy from their rival, the MacMillans.

Can these two overcome their rocky history and find love in the exclusive wealthy town of Somerset Harbor?

✅ Enemies to lovers office romance

✅ Sunny vs grumpy

✅ Billionaire romance

✅ Second chance

✅ Ex-high school bully

✅ Small exclusive wealthy town romance

With a sunny vs grumpy dynamic, a second chance at love, and a steamy enemies-to-lovers romance, Hate Mate is sure to leave you breathless.

This books is dedicated to those who seek revenge: may you find peace in forgiveness instead

They say revenge is a dish best served cold, but I've come to realize that love is a fire that can never be extinguished.

1

SAWYER

"What I would like to know is, if a man wants to expand his business, why does it take the approval of ten different people to do it?"

No matter how many times I say it out loud, it still boils my blood. My first big act as the new CEO of Somerset Harbor Yacht Club, and I need the approval of ten city officials. It's my business they're cutting into by dragging their feet.

"And it's your business. Why should they have a say in it?" My best friend Milo has never been much of a fan when it comes to following the rules. They're tiresome and boring. Naturally, that comment made him the perfect drinking companion tonight. Someone who I know will feed my righteous indignation.

I wave a hand, my gaze sweeping over the room. The very busy room, nestled in the yacht club my family owns. The club has been part of my life since I was born, but only now can I look over the gleaming bar and the club members enjoying their Thursday evening with a feeling of pride swelling in my chest. Now that Dad has stepped down and handed me the reins, everything looks different.

And I have to remember myself. The room is noisy, even with the doors leading out to the terrace wide open to let in the warm breeze, but not so loud that I want to take a chance that no one will hear the club's CEO bitching and moaning that his expansion plans have been put on hold for the time being.

“It's all a matter of where the new dining room is constructed,” I explain. “Locals don't want to block the view of the harbor, that sort of thing.”

He snorts before draining what's left in his glass. “You mean they want to be sure they can see their yacht from their front door?”

“Something like that.”

I lift a finger to Rich, the bartender, and he hustles our way from the other end of the bar. “Can I get you two, another?" he asks, eyeing our empty glasses.

"Please." I need to take it easy, though. No matter how good two glasses of whiskey feel after a frustrating day, I promised my father I would be a good boy. Even though he's in the Virgin Islands, his influence hangs over me. I wouldn't dare say that out loud to Milo, though, and not only because I don't admit things like that to anybody. Milo's got his own issues with his father when it comes to work, and I don't want to get him started.

As it turns out, he manages to find a way to steer the conversation in that direction. "It was the same way when I tried to get the permit for that multifamily project, remember?"

"The condos."

How could I forget? The idea nearly threw Somerset Harbor into a second civil war, all because Milo had the idea for his father's private equity firm to fund a new building downtown.

"The audacity of wanting to change things even the slightest bit," he grumbles, still bitter more than eight months later. "And then, when we can't get the permits and everything falls through, who does my father blame?"

"He didn't blame you specifically."

"Easy for you to say. You're not the one he's been staring at in disappointment for years. There's what he says, and there's what he really means. Never confuse the two." As soon as Rich slides a fresh whiskey his way, Milo bolts it back. So he's going to be in that kind of mood tonight.

"That's exactly the problem," I agree, rattling the ice in my glass when I lift it to my lips. The whiskey is smooth, warming me inside. "Narrow minds. Fear of change. I'm not suggesting we paint the building neon green and start holding mud wrestling competitions on Sunday afternoons. All I want is to expand the dining room. Now all I have is a lump of red tape where my plans should be."

"It's a matter of time. They'll drag their feet, but they'll give you what you want."

"Only if I kiss the ring," I remind him, sipping my whiskey again. It goes down smoother every time. "Do you know how it makes me grit my teeth to think about doing that?"

"You never did like to kiss ass," he points out.

"Who does? Politics, Dad calls it. I didn't get into politics. I got into owning a business that, might I add, have added quite a bit to the local economy over the years. You would think that would earn me a little bit of leeway."

"Maybe they'll want to play ball once your father's back from his trip."

Reflexively, my fingers close tighter around the glass, until I have no choice but to bolt the rest of its contents back in one quick motion. "I don't need him to make this happen," I remind my friend before slapping the glass onto the bar.

"Oh, no, I didn't mean it that way." It doesn't matter. He said it. And it was exactly what he meant.

He doesn't get it, though. It isn't that I've spent my life expecting to one day be the CEO of the club. I'm not a case of the spoiled billionaire's son with the silver spoon in his mouth walking through a life that's been plotted out for him, expecting everyone and everything to fall at his feet simply because that's the way his life has gone from day one.

I feel more at home here than I do in my own apartment. There's something about the smell of the place. The way my footsteps ring out on the floors. Soft conversation at lunchtime in the dining room, the sounding of horns in the harbor as guests arrive, docking their sailboats before strolling down the dock in anticipation of dinner with friends. The bustle of the kitchen, the laughter at the bar. This is my home.

I want to do right by my home and the people who visit my home, sometimes every day. That's the entire reason we need to expand in the first place—we're finding our members are taking more of their meals at the club, sometimes several days a week. It's getting to the point where we're booked solid most nights, sometimes turning away walk-ins because we don't have the room.

I hate like hell to lose that business, especially with the Macmillans building a new resort. Once that's complete, people will have somewhere else to go when we can't fit them in—and they might decide not to come back.

But if the city council insists on dragging its feet, it might be too late by the time we're up and running in our expanded dining room.

Again I signal Rich, because why the hell not? When's the last time I treated myself to a night without responsibilities? That's all life has been since Dad appointed me.

I don't resent it. I knew what I was getting into—but sometimes a man needs to let loose before he explodes.

I never used to have this problem, but then I wasn't exactly practiced in the art of self-restraint. Not when it came to enjoying myself. And throughout my twenties I did a lot of that. Maybe more than my fair share. So much so that at the age of twenty-nine, I feel old. Been there, done that. Jaded is the word for it. And tired.

Which is part of the reason why, when I catch Milo eyeing a curvy blonde at the other end of the bar, I grumble quietly to myself. All I wanted tonight was to bitch with a good friend and let off some steam.

I elbow him, hoping to bring the conversation back around. "I wonder if this is some kind of a test, after all," I muse before accepting the next round.

Milo looks my way, confused. "A test? What kind of test?"

"You mentioned my old man. I wonder if that's part of what this is about. I wonder if they ever made things as difficult for him."

"A bunch of small-minded assholes," he mutters. The lights shining behind the bar illuminate his stony expression as he leans in to grab his drink.

"I swear, it's like some of them are from a different century," I agree, and the two of us laugh. "I mean, you should hear the way they talk."

"That's why I wanted to get the hell out of here and go to New York."

"You should have—no, we both should have," I decide. "They think just because they've got money, that makes up for a lack of education. You can't even have a proper conversation with half of the people around here. They think just because they live near New York, it gives them class."

"Yeah, they're so cultured." We both roll our eyes, laughing.

"Add to that a bunch of city officials who don't know their heads from a hole in the ground, and you've got Somerset Harbor." We raise our glasses, laughing bitterly as we clink them together. Really, I have to laugh or dissolve into depression.

"I bet you could put the screws to them if you tried." Milo decides as he finishes his drink in a hurry. His gaze keeps drifting back to the blonde, who by now has noticed us. I'd have to be blind not to notice the appraising look she gives me, the way her lips curve in a smile. Plump, glossy lips that might feel damn good sliding up and down my—

Nope. I need to quit that train of thought before it leads in the wrong direction. Yet another promise I made to Dad: not using the female clientele as a personal dating pool. He was pretty serious about that one. He didn't need to warn me, really. I tend to be a one-and-done sort of guy, meaning there's not usually any follow-up date once I've slept with a woman.

That's not stopping Milo, though, who picks up his drink and jerks his chin. "Come on. I want to meet that girl."

"You're more than welcome to," I mutter.

"I need a wingman. I would do it for you."

He's right. He would do that for me. And the blonde is with a few friends who might appreciate a little attention while he takes all of hers.

It's going to be a long night.

2

WILLOW

"Are there any questions about the plan?"

The pair of young men seated across from my desk exchange completely clueless looks. It's almost enough to wipe the professional smile from my face, but I grit my teeth and maintain the expression. Here I was, thinking I had dumbed it down to the point where a small child could understand the steps I need these two to take if there's any hope of salvaging their reputation and their business.

Clearly, I didn't go quite far enough.

"So, what you're saying is, we can't go on any social media. At all."

"That's right," I murmur, frowning a little. "And I know that's a big ask."

"The biggest," they mutter almost in sync. Twins are like that, or so I've been told. Adam and Andrew, YouTube stars who have a bad habit of recording even the most intimate parts of their lives such as what turned out to be a drunken orgy with a bunch of girls on a party boat. Considering a lot of their content is mostly viewed by prepubescent boys who love video games, there's been something of an outcry from concerned parents.

"Of course, you need to create your content," I amend. "Content which will be edited and shared by your team. But nothing personal, not for at least a few weeks."

"How are we supposed to do that?" Andy demands. "That's how we keep our followers engaged."

Adam nods. "Yeah, do you know how much we could lose if we stop posting every day on TikTok and Insta?"

"And do you know how much you could lose if you post the wrong things?" There's a lot I could say about neither of them having good sense when it comes to what is and isn't appropriate, but

I do want to keep them as clients. Even a difficult, rather clueless client is valuable.

"Once your new social media manager comes on board, they will train you in what you can share and what you absolutely, under no circumstances should not. But since it will be a few weeks before they're able to get started, it's better for you to go radio silent except for business related content. That's all. This is not permanent." I look from one of them to the other, noting the way they even scowl in a similar way. "We're thinking long term, remember. We need to salvage your brand. Your new manager will help you create your family-friendly content."

"Long-term," Adam snickers. "The internet moves fast. We might not have a long-term."

"You'll be fine," I assure him. It isn't that I don't see his point. But like many nineteen-year-olds, they think in terms of the here and now. It's not always easy to see the big picture.

Add in the millions of dollars a month they now make and you have a recipe for trouble.

"I'm sure if you follow the steps I've outlined, everything will be just fine. But of course," I add, pushing my chair away from my desk and standing, "if you have any questions, don't hesitate to call me right away."

"Is it okay if we just text?" Andy asks.

"Sure thing." I'm not even that much older than they are, but it might as well be one or two generations between us.

Once I've ushered them through the waiting room and out of the office, I close the door behind them and touch my forehead to the cool wood, releasing a deep sigh. Soft laughter from the office situated across from mine floats my way. "Another lovely morning with the brain-dead twins?"

I turn around, leaning my back against the door. "I swear, I don't think they share a brain between the two of them. Yet here they are, making more money this month than I'll make all year."

"Social media is funny like that," Sarah muses, emerging from her office with a take-out container in each hand. "Just in time for lunch."

"Thank God. I'm starving." We head back into my office, and instead of sitting behind the desk I plop down on the leather sofa across the opposite wall. "Did they remember to put the dressing on the side this time?"

"Yes, ma'am." Sure enough, there's a container of blue cheese on top of my spinach salad. I can already smell the bacon and grilled chicken inside, and the aroma is enough to make my mouth water.

"I've never seen anybody look at a salad the way you do," Sarah muses, sitting down with her sausage and pepper sandwich. How she manages to eat like she does and still stay so skinny is a mystery. I love a good salad, but if I could get away with eating a greasy sandwich for lunch and not feel like a slug afterward, I would toss it out the window.

"Remind me why we decided to open up a PR firm," I murmur as I pop the lid on my dressing.

"Do you realize you ask me that question two or three times a week?"

"And you have yet to give me a solid answer," I retort. She sticks her tongue out at me before opening her mouth wider to fit as much of the sandwich in as possible. The girl is a blonde-haired, blue-eyed Amazonian goddess and she eats like a long-haul trucker. Some people are simply blessed.

When she's finished with her bite, I hand her a napkin and point to the corner of her mouth. "I mean, I know we're good at what we do. We have strategic minds."

"Mm-hmm," she agrees while chewing.

"But having to grin and bear it when some of these idiots question us? I mean, look at the twins. They post a graphic, drug-fueled party and have the nerve to challenge *me*. The professional, the expert they came to for help."

Finally she swallows, nodding. "I know. It's baffling. Like, why did you come here if you're not going to listen?"

"Exactly."

"But most of the clients are good."

"Sure, for the most part, they listen. They know what they're paying for. They can appreciate experience."

"Try getting that from a pair of nineteen-year-old internet sensations."

"Exactly. Thank God it's Friday."

The truth is working with my best friend makes all of this a lot more fun. Our daily lunches and the way we can call out to each other from our offices when there are no clients around. We know each other and understand each other's rhythms. We know when to pick up the slack when the other is not at their best.

She pulls out her phone and starts scrolling, and I can't help but indulge my curiosity. "What's so interesting?"

Her cheeks darken before she slides me an embarrassed glance. "Sorry. No offense. I wanted to see if somebody I matched with sent me a message yet."

"I thought you deleted the dating apps from your phone."

"Yeah, well, the thing about apps is you can always download them again."

"Sarah..."

"Hey, not all of us can be okay with being on our own the way you are."

That stings, though I do my best to hide it. "Who said I was okay with it?"

"You know what I mean. You're the only person I know who doesn't actively try to date."

"Because I'm actively building a business, remember?" I do my best to laugh it off while stabbing a piece of chicken harder than I need to.

"Well believe me, you're not missing anything."

I stick to my salad, afraid of sounding sharp or irritated if I say anything else. Sarah has been my best friend since our days at Penn, and we see eye-to-eye on just about everything. Really, if there is such a thing as soul mates, she's the one. I've never met another friend who could look at me and instantly know what's going on in my head.

At the same time, there are moments like this when she doesn't think before speaking. She assumes I am actively trying to avoid relationships when truly, I don't have the time to put into it. Nobody wants to date someone who is only ever half-present, constantly juggling client meetings at all hours of the day and night depending on the severity of the latest emergency.

"I'm glad you can find enough balance in your life to think about dating," I murmur, picking at the leaves so I don't have to reveal my discomfort. I don't know why that set me off like it did. Just one of those things you don't know bothers you until it comes up.

"You could, too," she reasons. "If you weren't such a control freak. And you know I say that with love. Sometimes, though, you need to learn to let go a little bit. You can't work all day, every day. You're going to burn out, and then what happens to me? I lose my best friend and my business partner."

She sticks out her bottom lip in a parody of a pout. "Please, won't you think of me?"

"You're such a jerk." But I have to laugh. What she's saying comes from a good place, and she's right about my control freak tendencies. I can't help it. I like structure in my life, which means socializing and dating are a curveball I can't always manage. It's hard to predict what happens tomorrow or next week or even later today when I add in other people, outside factors. Most of the time, I would rather spend a night with my laptop.

That, I can predict. That, I can manage.

A ping from my phone signals a new email. "You're on your lunch break," Sarah reminds me to no avail. I'm already reaching for the thing, opening the app, tucking a strand of dark hair behind my ear before I begin to read.

"What is it?" she asks in a hushed voice when my eyes go wide and my mouth falls open.

"I'm still not quite sure," I confess, reading the message again. "But if it's what I think it is, this day has just gotten a lot more interesting."

3

SAWYER

It's a nightmare. It's a complete goddamn nightmare. If I set out to destroy my professional reputation and the fate of my family's club, I couldn't have done better than I did last night.

At least Dad is in the islands. That is literally the only redeeming aspect of this entire situation.

It was bad enough I woke up this morning feeling like a truck ran me over at some point last night. I eventually lost count of the drinks I slung back, so it came as no surprise that even though I downed some ibuprofen and a ton of water before falling into bed, a brass band was in the middle of a symphony when I opened my eyes. I'm not as young as I used to be—nights like that don't roll off my back anymore. There was a time I would have jumped out of bed, downed a Gatorade, and moved on with my life.

If only that was the biggest problem I had to face.

When I checked my phone out of habit, the sight of two dozen missed calls and another dozen text messages left all thoughts of a hangover in the dust. It was Milo who ended up filling me in, as he was the one who called me the most. My brothers contributed a call or two, but it was Milo blowing my phone up for two hours before I ever lifted an eyelid.

Right away, he barked a question. “Who was near us last night?”

My head threatened to split open at the way he shouted. “What?”

“Who did you see near us at the bar? Did you recognize them?”

I closed my eyes and tried to put myself back in the situation, but I came up blank. *At least I know this isn’t about Dad getting sick or having an accident.* It was my only consolation. “What's this all about?”

“I texted you a video. Watch it, then call me back.” He ended the call before I could ask any more questions.

That video. My stomach turns to ice at the thought of it. I've watched it dozens of times today, maybe a hundred. Over and over I've replayed it, until I have every word memorized.

"You should hear how they talk!" God, I sounded like such a half-drunken asshole. "They think just because they've got money, that makes up for their lack of education."

Me. Milo. Every word of our bitch session was recorded. My face was completely clear, and anyone familiar with the club could identify the bar in a heartbeat. Whoever the videographer is, they're skilled at taking a crystal-clear video without being spotted.

After watching it again, I called Milo back, my hands shaking, nausea threatening to overtake me. "What the hell is that?"

"What does it look like? Somebody recorded every word."

"Where did you find it?"

"A friend of mine sent it to me. She got it from Twitter. She said it had already been retweeted a bunch of times, and that was two hours ago."

Thus began what is shaping up to be one of the worst days of my life. It's far and away the worst day of my professional life, no doubt, but my personal life is bound to take a steep nose dive the second Dad gets wind of this.

Hours later, seated in my office, there's nothing I can do but watch the numbers tick upward, slowly but surely. The number of people commenting, retweeting. No, this isn't exactly worldwide news, and I doubt people even as nearby as New York or Boston would hear about it or even care very much if they did.

But here in Somerset Harbor? It's a different story. It's a small world, and people do love to talk.

Calling down to the dining room at noon, I ask, "How are our reservations for this evening?"

Considering it's a Friday, we ought to be in good shape, booked solid.

The hostess on duty keeps me waiting a moment or two before she lets out something between a groan and a whimper.

"It looks like we've had a handful of cancellations for this evening," she finally reports, speaking slowly and carefully.

No. This isn't happening. We had to turn guests away last Friday night, we were so busy. "How much is a handful?"

"Since this morning, there have been eight cancellations." She pauses, taking a deep breath. "And there were a few more for lunch, too."

"How is it down there right now?" My office is not on the ground level, so there's no way for me to know without either calling down or taking the elevator myself. Considering I dread facing a single local for fear of what they've heard, this is the safest way to find out.

"We have customers," she tells me.

My eyes close, and the same sick feeling that's haunted me all morning intensifies. She doesn't have to spell it out. Already, people have gotten word, and they're pissed.

Who could blame them? Even if they haven't watched the video themselves, they know I called them all a bunch of morons with no education, class, or intelligence. I don't even know what the hell I was thinking—my ego and wounded pride were doing the talking for me. Unfortunately, I doubt that will serve as much consolation to a bunch of insulted citizens who would much rather spend their money where they feel appreciated and respected.

After thanking the hostess for her help, I close my eyes and rub my temples. What am I going to do?

Dad finds out about this and I'm screwed. Goodbye CEO. Hello family disappointment.

Think, think. It's the perfect storm, really. Not only did I make a world-class jackass out of myself last night, but I'm still dealing with a hangover that leaves my brain feeling like mush. I can't think fast enough when that's exactly what I need to do. I need to think fast.

My brothers will never let me live this one down, that much is for sure. So far, I've managed to avoid returning their calls. Brooks has called me the most, and considering he's our events manager, he has good reason to be concerned. Thank God he's out of town for a few days so there's no risk of him storming in here. I can't bring myself to respond to his calls, not yet. I want to have at least the faintest outline of a plan in place to make up for this before I take my medicine and get dressed down by my younger brother.

Overnight, I've gone from a respected business owner to a pariah who managed to insult and alienate the people who pay our bills. How do I come back from this? And how do I do it quickly enough that Dad won't find out? There I was, worried at first when he announced he'd go no contact during his trip. Now I see his decision as my only hope of salvation. If I can get this cleaned up before he returns, I can move on from it.

And that's when it hits me. Jayden.

"Please pick up," I whisper after pulling up his contact and placing a call. "Please, pick up, man."

"Sawyer, what's up?"

I nearly collapse with relief at the sound of his voice. "I've got a problem. Not to bring up bad memories," I murmur, "but I need the contact info for that PR specialist you used."

"Oh. You get in a little trouble? I told you to stop sleeping around with the daughters of your club members."

I wish it were something as incidental as what he's describing. "Yeah, you know me. I have to learn my lessons the hard way. Do you have her number?"

"Sure thing. I'll text it over to you, along with her email."

"Thank you so much. I'm sorry, I don't have a lot of time to talk. I need to get through to her right away." He sounds understanding as we end the call, and not half a minute later a text comes through with the contact information.

I can only hope she's as good for me as she was for him. Considering he got caught making a donation to a charity that turned out to be the front for a terrorist group and she was able to squelch the entire scandal in no time, I feel a reasonable amount of hope.

This isn't quite as scandalous as that, but it's pretty damn close. Especially in this town.

Willow Anderson. Normally I'd go a little internet sleuthing, check out her LinkedIn profile or something like that if only to get a look at her. There's no time for that now. I instantly open a new email on my MacBook and begin typing out a quick but urgent plea for a meeting. I don't care what it takes. I don't care what her rate is. Money is no object at a time like this.

"Willow," I whisper before sending off the e-mail, "I hope you're as good as you're supposed to be."

All the while, my phone continues to buzz with missed calls and messages. A constant reminder of what happens when I make the mistake of combining alcohol with feeling sorry for myself.

This Willow had better be on her game, or else I might as well kiss my business—and my father's opinion of me—goodbye.

4

WILLOW

"I still can't believe my eyes," I confess to Sarah after reading the email a few times. It's still the same. Nothing has changed. Do I expect it to?

Turning to her, I can't help but laugh—high-pitched, a little giddy. "I mean, is this really happening? Do things like this happen in real life? Maybe I invented it."

Sarah, meanwhile, is still in the dark even if she laughs at my choice of words. She's in the dark mostly because I can't accurately explain the situation with an absolute frenzy going on in my head. A frenzy set off by the sight of his name. Sawyer Cargill.

Just the thought of him makes me regret eating lunch once my stomach starts churning. Like the memory of the man attached to that heinous name is enough to set off a storm inside me.

"I would really love a little insight," she reminds me, polishing off her sandwich.

Wallowing Willow. It's been more than a decade since anyone's used the charming little nickname he came up with back when I was overweight, with frizzy hair and acne, yet all the old feelings come rushing back. It might as well have happened yesterday, all the bullying and teasing and alienating.

Get it together. You are a grown, professional woman now.

"This is an email from Sawyer Cargill," I explain. Even my voice is trembling, but not from pain or discomfort. More like excitement, and a lot of it. "He needs my help."

"Sawyer... wait." Her mouth falls open, her eyes going wide. "Wasn't he the one you told me about?"

"So you remember." Yet another one of the benefits of working with my best friend: we know each other's history, drastically cutting down on the amount of time it takes to fill the other in on a situation like this. When we first met back at Penn as roommates, Sawyer was recent history and the wounds were fresh. I had to explain at first why I had a hard time putting myself out there and meeting new people. Incredible, the wounds a thoughtless bully can inflict. I'm sure he never paid me a moment's thought past the last time we set eyes on each other.

"No offense, but that's not the kind of story a girl forgets. He made life hell for you back in the day."

"He made life hell for a lot of people. I was just one of many."

Her brows draw together before she scowls. "Okay, but you happen to be my best friend, so you're the one I care a little more about."

I can't argue with that. "Do you know how many times I have fantasized about this kind of thing happening? I mean, granted, he was usually begging for my forgiveness on hands and knees, crawling over broken glass, that sort of thing. But this is much better."

"What does he say?"

I clear my throat, forcing back cackles of pure glee. "Ms. Anderson, you come highly recommended by a friend of mine with whom you worked in the recent past. He has nothing but good things to say about your skills—considering you got him out of an ugly situation regarding money he contributed to what turned out to be a terrorist group, it was no small feat."

"Oh! He must be talking about that Jayden guy."

"Probably," I murmur before continuing. "Unfortunately, I got myself into trouble thanks to my big mouth and a bystander recording my frustrations toward the citizens of my small town —Somerset Harbor. It's a bit of a disaster that threatens to destroy my family's business thanks to the video making the rounds and catching the eye of the wrong people. Please, I need to make this go away immediately, and you're the only person who can help."

The only person who can help. I can't pretend those words don't stir a thrill in my chest, roughly in the area where my wounded heart sits. It's strange, really. Here I am, the owner of a business which is evidently successful enough that word has spread even to someone as wealthy and connected as Sawyer Cargill, yet I might as well be seventeen again. He has a strange way of turning back the clock. Taking me right back to the old days when he and his nasty little circle of friends made it their business to humiliate and make miserable anybody who didn't rise to their standards. I certainly qualified.

I almost expect to look down and find myself wearing a private school uniform—that plaid, pleated skirt never was my favorite piece of clothing. But now, I'm wearing the same suit I wore for my meeting with the twins and a pair of red soled Louboutin pumps. I've come a long way from those days. I need to remember who I am, not who I was.

But do we ever really change? The outside might improve, but the inside? Those scars don't magically dissolve just because a girl now straightens her frizzy hair.

"Are you okay over there?" Sarah's question brings me back to reality, reminding me I am not that girl anymore. I'm a woman with another decade of living under my belt. I'm sitting in a skyscraper in the heart of New York City, and the invoice those two kids are going to receive after our meeting symbolizes more money than I had ever seen all at once back in the day. Back when I found out simply being accepted to a private school and being able to afford it thanks to a scholarship were not enough to buy entrance into a very rarefied, elite group of people. I was never going to be one of them, despite the uniform.

"I'm fine," I tell her, grinning wickedly to myself. Staring out the window, imagining the possibilities thanks to this simple email.

"The tables sure have turned, haven't they?"

My head bobs up and down. "And of course, he wouldn't remember me," I muse. "I doubt he ever knew my last name."

"Then again, if he did even half of the things you've described, he's probably too ashamed of himself to bring it up."

"I don't think he possesses the gene that makes shame possible." All I see in my mind's eye is his roguish smirk, the light that danced in his brown eyes whenever he was reinforcing his superiority over me and the rest of the underdogs. There weren't many of us, but that only shone a brighter spotlight on those who didn't fit in.

"Could be—in which case, he's got a lot of balls, coming to you for help."

"If there's one thing I've learned from working with our clients," I point out while turning my attention back to her, "it's what little introspection some of them possess. When you've grown up in a world where nothing you do has any real consequences, I guess you don't think about how your actions are going to affect the people around you. And believe me, Sawyer grew up with more money than God. I would be surprised if this is the only skeleton in his closet."

"Well, now you have the chance to tell him to screw himself."

Is it wrong that a little thrill of excitement races through me at the idea? After all these years. I'm finally going to get the chance to tell him exactly what I think about him. How hilarious it is to me that he's doing exactly what he always said he didn't want to do back in school: following in his father's footsteps, running the family business, bowing and scraping to a bunch of dusty old people—his words, not mine. He's so pitiful, he couldn't be bothered to step out on his own and make a name for himself. It was much easier to sit back and wait for his father to retire so he could take the reins and continue living life on easy mode.

But life isn't so easy, is it? "I have no doubt his big mouth got him into trouble," I muse, skimming the message again like there is a chance it will say something different this time. "All he ever did was run his mouth back in the day."

"And you can remind him of that. I am seriously jealous of you." She holds up her clenched fists, shadow boxing. "Punch him right in the balls.

Make him feel it for all of us who never got the chance."

I can't help but roll my eyes. "Please. You've been walking this earth looking like a supermodel from day one."

Her face falls a little, and I instantly regret my choice of words.

"There are still mean people in the world," she reminds me in a softer voice. "Jerks and idiots and men who ghost you after stringing you along for weeks."

The way she says it, she's speaking from experience.

"You're right. I'm sorry."

I sink back against the supple leather, taking in my surroundings, looking at them from a fresh perspective. The tasteful decor, the amazing view outside my window. This is my business, something I built, and I'm a success. The sky's the limit when it comes to how far I can go. I've got something to be proud of, something worth respecting.

I don't need to hang on to those memories. I can put all of that behind me. Sawyer can dangle on a thread for all I care, kicking his feet to avoid touching them to the fire blazing under him. I'm not even required to offer a response.

But wouldn't it be nice to get a little closure before I move on once and for all?

"Uh-oh."

"What?" I ask her.

"You're grinning. I know that look. You just got an idea."

Lifting a shoulder, I try, and fail, to hide a smirk. "Maybe I should go to an interview."

If her eyebrows go any higher, they might leave her forehead entirely. "Are you sure?"

"Yeah. I think so." Now there's no hiding my wicked smile while my heart begins to flutter in anticipation. "It might not be a bad idea to see him face-to-face one more time and tell him exactly what I think about him."

"So long as you're sure it's the right thing for you."

"Don't worry," I tell her, my smile widening as everything starts coming together in my head. "I think I have a plan."

5

SAWYER

What is taking her so long? What kind of hotshot is she supposed to be that she can't be bothered to answer a simple email in a timely fashion? I should have called her in the first place—that was my fault. I should have gotten her on the phone and told her the story first hand rather than turn my emergency into just another email she can discard.

That, and the other three messages I've sent this afternoon alone. I need her to understand how vital it is that we get this taken care of immediately. I would call her now, but I'm too busy having my ass handed to me in an emergency board meeting.

Quickly I type out one last Hail Mary of a message and send it before I can talk myself out of it. ***Please, Ms. Anderson, I am ready to do whatever it is you think is best, and money is no object. I'm in desperate need of your help.***

Because what's the use of posturing? I'm on the verge of losing everything that's ever mattered, so why not throw my pride in on top of everything else? It isn't like I have much left, seated before a board comprised of men my father's age, all of whom stare at me with the same look of disapproval.

This is my club, damn it, yet they behave like they own the place. I practically grew up inside these walls, playing beneath the very conference table around which we now sit. Doesn't that count for anything?

No—in fact, I get the feeling my history at the club might work against me. They still see me as that little kid, not as the man I've grown into. And they've been waiting for the opportunity to express their opinions without Dad around to temper their reactions.

"Sawyer, this is extremely disappointing." Michael Harris, one of Dad's oldest friends, sits to my right. He might be the most sympathetic of all of them, and still his comment stings. Maybe because I can easily imagine those words coming from my father if he were here.

"As I've already expressed, I accept full responsibility for what happened. I was unaware there was someone recording my conversation, but it's no excuse. I should have been more discreet."

"You should have kept your mouth shut," fires back good old Nathan Fields, the board's Chairman, who glares at me from the other end of the conference table. "It was a damn childish thing to do."

Someone needs to remind this man that just because he's known me since I was a child gives him no right to speak to me as if I were still wearing braces. "Respectfully, are you speaking for yourself right now, or for my father? Because I can already imagine very clearly what he'd have to say if he were here."

He grumbles, shaking his bald head. "After all the work your family has put into this club."

"Not to mention the damage this will do to your reputation in town," Michael murmurs, far kinder but no less serious. "A business like this relies on goodwill more than nearly anything else. You are the symbol of the club. A jovial, welcoming host. A friend."

Nathan pounds the side of his fist against the heavy table at which he's sat for countless meetings over the years. "Yes, and who wants to be the friend of a man who looks down on them and considers them uncultured, uneducated?" There's a lot of grumbling, and I have to wonder if these men took it personally. I wasn't speaking of any of them in particular, but a hit dog will holler. They clearly took it hard, imagining I was talking about them.

"When your father decided to step aside and put you in his position, I have to admit, I had my reservations." Nathan's observation is met with soft muttering from the others, who may not have agreed at the time but will certainly pretend like they did now that it suits them.

If I grind my teeth much harder, they'll crack. "I understand."

"But he assured me," Nathan continues as if I never spoke, "that you were mature enough and responsible enough to take this on. He told me you understood the weight of this role, that you were keen on continuing the family's legacy."

"And he was right."

"I have to wonder now." He sits back in his chair, shaking his head once again. Much more of that, and he'll end up with a crick in his neck. "If you were older, I might be able to more easily understand how you could be so irresponsible."

"I'm not sure I know what you mean."

Waving a dismissive hand, he explains. "Those of our generation aren't so accustomed to people around them holding recording devices at all times. Now more than ever, it's vital to be aware of your surroundings and to know how easy it is for everything you say and do to become fodder for gossip and speculation."

This gets worse by the minute. Meanwhile, my phone has not so much as buzzed to announce a new message. *Come on, Willow*. There are other PR firms in New York, of course, but she's the one with the proven track record. I don't have time to interview others, to ask around about their results.

Meanwhile, the men seated before me expect me to continue groveling until it suits them. "The only thing I can offer is, it was a mistake. And I'm doing everything I can to rectify the situation."

"Exactly what are you doing?" asks Paul Snyder, sitting at Nathan's right hand. I've always thought of him as a stuck up little yes man, the sort of guy who trails around in the shadows of bigger, more confident men.

"Yes," grunts Frank Bruno, seated across from Paul and staring through me with eyes that seem to burn. "What are you doing? Is there a plan in place?" Considering this only broke hours ago, he's asking for a lot.

"I am..." Pulling my phone from my pocket, I check just in case but am disappointed once again. It takes effort to hide my reaction in front of a hostile crowd. "I'm currently in talks with a handful of public relations firms in the city. I should have something in place by the end of the day."

"Oh?" Nathan asks, sitting up straight again. "Who did you have in mind? I'm familiar with a few of the firms out there."

My stomach sinks while the eyes of every other man in the room bore holes into me. It takes everything I have not to squirm visibly under their scrutiny.

"It doesn't matter," Paul interjects, sparing me the agony of trying to come up with a response. After all, there's only one firm I'm interested in, and I doubt anyone would be impressed if they knew I haven't cast a wider net. "What could you possibly do to make up for this? You should have sent out a statement this morning as soon as that damn video circulated."

"I would rather not take a step like that until I have a professional's advice," I counter. "I don't want to make any further missteps."

"Fine. Meanwhile, the longer you wait to decide who's worthy of working with you, the worse this gets. We could end up with a failed business on our hands because of this. Doesn't that matter to you?"

My blood was already at a low simmer. Every word this little runt throws at me ups the temperature.

"You know it matters," I murmur, clenching my fists out of sight beneath the table. "It matters very much. And there are only so many ways I can express my regret. I'm going to do everything in my power to make this right. I was drunk and insulting—but I would like to look around this table and ask if there's one of you who hasn't spoken out of turn when they were in that condition."

"There's a single, glaring difference," Nathan counters. "None of us were in the position you were in. You employ many dozens of people, and even more during the spring and summer months. This is about more than reputation and legacy. You have a responsibility. And I shudder to think how your father will feel about this when he gets word."

Bullseye. And he knows it, the smug, superior prick.

I am a grown man. Well past the days when the threat of telling Daddy on me should have an effect.

Yet the slightest mention of him and the disappointment I know he would express leaves me sweating, anxious. After sipping water, I murmur, "As you know, my father has gone no contact. I don't know even how to reach him—and believe me, my brothers and I expressed concern, but you know how he is when he gets an idea in his head."

"I guess that makes it convenient for you," Frank mutters.

"Considering my father is at an age where I would rather be in touch with him at all times in case something should happen, I don't consider it convenient at all." After a brief, tense staring contest, he looks away first. The sanctimonious idiot.

"I think we should put it to a vote." Charles Moran is seated to my left, and he slides a knowing look my way. He's never been a supporter of mine, putting it mildly. I'll never forget him suggesting the board take over leadership of the club until I was better prepared to step into this role. I'm sure he is loving this—hell, he's not even trying very hard to hide his amusement, grinning slightly when our eyes meet.

"And what would you be voting on?" I ask, gritting my teeth once again. It would be so easy to wrap my hands around his throat and squeeze.

"On whether the board should step in and take control of the situation while you get yourself straightened out." He waves a dismissive hand. "We know what to do and say to get the town back on board and smooth any ruffled feathers."

"That's right," Frank agrees. "Let's get the upper hand before this blows any further out of proportion. As it is, I heard of nothing else all morning. Everywhere I went, people were talking about this."

That's because nobody around here has anything better to talk about.

When my phone buzzes, I know how it must feel to be adrift at sea and out of nowhere be thrown a life preserver. My hands are shaking as I open the email app and find the one name I wanted more than anything to see in my inbox.

"Excuse me, gentleman." I realize I'm holding my breath as I open the message. *Please, please, tell me what I need to hear.*

Mr. Cargill, I would be happy to meet with you and discuss your needs. While I cannot make promises regarding whether we would make a good fit, I have handled situations like this before and believe it might be possible to sweep all of this under the rug with little complication. However, we would need to start immediately, which means a sit down meeting at the earliest possible convenience.

It's all-encompassing, the wave of relief that washes over me and almost steals the breath from my lungs. I'm practically weak with it, while at the same time I want to laugh. Thank God. There might actually be a way to get out of this with my hide intact.

The men grumble among themselves while I do my best to regain my composure. "This is good news," I tell them, forcing myself to smile in the face of their scrutiny.

"I don't know how familiar any of you are with Willow Anderson, but she heads an office out of Manhattan and worked miracles for a friend of mine who became entangled with a terrorist front he believed was a worthwhile charity. She comes very highly recommended, in other words, and she has agreed to take me on as a client."

A few of the men sigh in relief, but not Nathan. His penetrating gaze never wavers, to the point where I have to force myself to look him in the eye without flinching. "It's been confirmed, then? You will be working together?"

This jerk. No wonder he and my father get along so well. I could jump through rings of fire and it wouldn't be enough. "Yes, indeed. I have the message right here. We're getting together first thing in the morning, and before the weekend's over we'll roll out a plan."

Rings of fire? Right now, I feel more like I'm tap dancing for my life, putting on a smile and hoping it's enough to distract them from the fact that I have two left feet.

“I'm sure services like that don't come cheap,” he muses, pursing his lips in false concern.

I know exactly what he's getting at, and it's enough to make me want to scream. “I will be paying for this out of pocket,” I assure all of them while staring straight at him. “This is my problem. I wouldn't take the money from the club, you can believe me on that.”

I never considered taking the funds from the business. It's one thing to know your presence was never exactly welcome. It's another to find out exactly how little people think of you. I have to wonder what I’ve ever done to inspire such a lack of confidence, not to mention their low opinion of my character.

“None of us believed otherwise,” Michael assures me, but I have my doubts. Doubts that are confirmed when Paul and Nathan exchange a knowing glance.

“So I think we can all agree,” I continue, forcing myself to ignore them, “there is no need to disrupt my father's well-deserved peace and relaxation by trying to get a hold of him. It's a non-issue.”

“We'll see,” Nathan murmurs, but I don't care once he pushes his chair back from the table. He can say whatever he wants, so long as he's out of my face.

"Everything's under control," I insist as the men pack it in. Those who stayed quietly supportive throughout the meeting settle for extending a sympathetic grimace while shaking my hand. At least it seems like I have a couple of them on my side, but not enough that their opinion would carry if it came to a vote. The last time I checked, four is greater than two.

"I will be sure to keep you in the loop," I promise as I usher the men out of our conference room, down the hall from my office. Only once they're all in the elevator with the doors sliding shut between us can I release the tension in virtually every muscle of my body, including my racing heart.

I didn't exactly tell the truth back there, but they never have to know that. All I needed was a foot in the door, and Willow granted me that much by responding favorably to my pleas. If I didn't know better, I would think she wanted me to beg for it before agreeing to meet with me.

A glance at my watch gets me moving quickly down the hall, where I already have everything packed up and ready to go. The family helicopter is waiting at the helipad in preparation for a previously scheduled meeting in the city. What a shame it took Willow so long to get back to me—we might have been able to work something out this evening, since I'll be in her backyard.

The driver is waiting for me outside, parked discreetly by the side of the building rather than in a more conspicuous place where guests might be able to see. I hate that I had to instruct him to do that, but I'm not taking any chances. I would rather not show my face if at all possible, not until this nightmare gets straightened out. If Willow Anderson is anywhere near as good as she's supposed to be, it shouldn't be much longer.

Though I'm not deluded. As soon as I'm settled in the car on the way to the helipad, I pull out my phone to compose a response.

Willow—thank you so much for your reply. I just got out of a meeting with my board, and suffice it to say I'll need to get started on this as soon as humanly possible. I would be eternally grateful if you could make it out here as early as tomorrow and would be glad to send my helicopter out for you if that would make things easier. Whatever you need.

Then, because I can't leave it there, I add, ***And so you know how extremely important this is,***

and how committed I am to working together, I would be glad to offer $200,000 for your services. Would that be enough to do the job properly? Please let me know if tomorrow will work for you, and what time I can expect you here at the club. I can't tell you what a relief it is to know I'll have you in my corner.

Because if there's one thing I've learned in this life, it's that you have to act *as if*. Act as if you have the job, as if you have the support you need, as if everything's going according to plan. It's the only way to get what you want. The world has a way of living up to the standards you set for it.

And while the thought of parting with almost a quarter of a million dollars doesn't exactly thrill me, I'm ready to do whatever it takes to make this happen. I will not lose what's mine all because of a moment of indiscretion. I will take this and I will learn from it. I will never put myself in this position again.

First, I need to come out a winner on the other side. The idea of standing in front of Nathan and the others while they vote to unseat me is unthinkable. When I look at it that way, two hundred grand seems a small price to pay to maintain my dignity and show that son of a bitch he's wrong, that Dad made the right decision by naming me as his replacement.

I am going to win, no matter what it takes. Because I do not lose.

Willow Anderson, you'd better be as good as I've heard, because you hold my future in your hands.

6

WILLOW

Every mile I travel on my way to Somerset Harbor widens my smile until I'm sure by the time I arrive, my face will ache and my jaw will be stiff.

But no matter how I try, I can't wipe it from my face. This is it. This is the moment teenage Willow prayed for. All alone, late at night, crying herself to sleep while wondering what she ever did to deserve the treatment she received. Like the time I made the unforgivable mistake of bumping into Sawyer while rushing to class. You'd think I broke his ribs, the way he acted. *"Watch out, everybody! There's a rhino on the rampage!"*

That wasn't even the worst. There was one night in particular I'll never forget as long as I live, when I wished I would die rather than face anybody ever again. He deserves this for that night alone if nothing else.

I am not that girl anymore, but here's the thing about being bullied, you never really forget. You might put it behind you, compartmentalize, lock it away. There could come a moment now or then when you witness someone else being bullied and all the old feelings bubble back up to the surface—anger, embarrassment, frustration, even rage. But then they go away again, because, after all, you have a life to live. A life that's ages away from the person you used to be.

Still, that part of yourself exists, and right now the old version of me is front and center. She wants me to drive faster, because after all she has waited long enough to have her say.

Two hundred thousand dollars. He's that desperate. Desperate to salvage his reputation, his business, his relationship with his daddy. Something tells me that's front and center in all of this, though I doubt he would ever admit it out loud.

In other words, I've got him by the balls. There are still times, like right this very minute, when I feel like I should pinch myself in case I'm dreaming. But then if I am dreaming, I don't want to wake up. Because when will I ever have the chance to experience this again? This completely random bit of synchronicity bringing us together again. What are the odds of him knowing a past client of mine? Of all the public relations experts in the world, I'm the one he reached out to.

And now, he's going to find out how it feels to be rejected.

Though I doubt I could ever make him feel exactly the way he made me feel. I don't think I have it in me to be that cruel. It takes a special kind of coldness. Yes, we were kids—I'll give him that. But he went out of his way to humiliate me.

My hands tighten around the wheel until the squeak of leather and the ache in my joints make me loosen up. I can't do this to myself, getting angry when I'm so close to town and the club. When I first set eyes on him, I want to be cool, calm, and collected. Professional. I want him to see exactly who he made the mistake of hurting. The woman I've become. A woman with the power to make or break him now.

In other words, he's going to become the poster boy for being careful about who you bully, because you might one day need them enough to offer two hundred grand for their services.

The ringing of my phone echoes through the car's sound system, and I reach out to touch the green button on the display when I see it's Sarah who's calling. "You said you'd call before you left," she complains when I answer.

"I know. I'm sorry, my blowout took longer than expected." Because obviously, I pulled out all the stops, booking an emergency appointment at both the nail salon and the Dry Bar before accepting Sawyer's request for a meeting today. I wasn't about to confirm before I made sure I could look my best.

A glance at myself in the rearview mirror serves as a reminder of how far I've come. No frizzy flyaways, no Coke bottle glasses making my eyes look twice as big as they are. My skin is clear now, my face carefully contoured. I look pretty damn good, in other words.

"Are you ready for this?" she asks. "I really think I should have come with you."

"No need for that," I insist in a gentle voice. "I've got it under control."

The strangled groan she can't silence makes me think she's unconvinced. "What if he says something to hurt your feelings? What if he's a complete tool?"

"I have no doubt he's that," I mutter while changing lanes to prepare for my upcoming exit. "It's, like, coded in his DNA."

"It might have been a better idea to have somebody there to speak for you if you get overwhelmed."

She is my best friend, and I love her dearly, but for some reason her concern sets my teeth on edge. "I'm afraid I might have given you the wrong idea," I explain as gently as I can. "This is going to be the shortest meeting in the history of meetings. He's going to beg for my help, and I'm going to turn him down. I'm going to take a few minutes to savor him dissolving into tears—five, at most—and then I'll leave. End of story."

"I'm sure he'll want to know why you're turning down such a ridiculous amount of money."

"Oh, and I have every intention of telling him exactly why," I assure her. No matter how confident I try to sound, the sight of the Somerset Harbor exit makes my pulse pick up speed.

"Just be careful," she warns. "We can't afford to have word getting out that we're unprofessional."

My heartbeat stutters a little. "Is that what you're worried about? I wouldn't do anything to jeopardize what we've built. I promise you." And now I feel bad that she even had to think that.

"I don't know why I even worried. I know you better than that."

"I will be a good girl, I promise. And I'll call you as soon as I finish up."

"But do me a favor?"

"Name it."

"Make sure he knows exactly why you're turning him down."

"I plan to. But in a nice way," I add in case she's still worried. Granted, I don't know for sure whether I'll be able to make good on it, but she doesn't need to know. "I'll let you know when it's over. Maybe we could go out tonight, grab some drinks to celebrate finally having closure."

She has no idea how many times I've practiced this in my head since yesterday afternoon. It's been less than twenty-four hours, but I have already gone through countless scenarios in my head. Sure, it would have been nice if I had gotten a little more sleep—my concealer is working overtime on the bags under my eyes—but I may as well be a little kid on Christmas Eve, eagerly awaiting morning. My brain was on overdrive, both anticipating our meeting and dreading it slightly.

I'm only human. Seeing in person the man who made me feel so small and insignificant is bound to stir up mixed emotions.

It wasn't enough that he went out of his way to make fun of me whenever our paths crossed at school. He couldn't leave it there, laughing at me with his friends, asking if my frizzy, uncontrollable curls were a wig, wondering out loud where I found a uniform as big as the one I needed to wear. Even my thick glasses were fodder for his extremely unfunny jokes.

I can still hear echoes of the nasty comments and the laughter from him and his so-called friends, and it makes my shoulders hunch up around my ears the way they did back then. *Breathe, girl. You've got this.*

Sure, I wasn't the only person he tormented. Anybody even slightly different was a target. Somehow, he seemed to take particular pleasure in taunting me, probably because I was no good at hiding my reactions. No matter how hard I fought, I couldn't keep from tearing up, which only made him laugh harder.

Nothing he did topped my humiliation at the senior dance.

Just thinking about it stirs nausea in my belly. That night, when I was so proud of myself. I'd spent every last penny I had on my dress, and its shimmery, full skirt made me feel like a princess when I zipped it up. I even managed to tame my mane into a soft cloud of curls pinned in place at the nape of my neck.

I felt pretty and classy as I sailed into the decorated gymnasium, my cheeks flushed with excitement. I was so sure everybody would see me through new eyes and wish they had been nicer to me.

And when Sawyer's eyes widened at the sight of me, I was sure I'd had the intended effect. No, I didn't have a crush on him—not really. That didn't mean it wouldn't have thrilled me to know he thought I looked good for once. For one brief moment, maybe one of the best moments of my young life, I thought I'd won. I'd made my bully see how wrong he was, how he had misjudged me. I was on top of the world.

And it only got better when he approached me toward the end of the night. Even now, the memory of the way he looked that night is crystal clear. Like any girl's dream come true. His brown eyes were warm and friendly for once, and his generous mouth was set in what looked like a genuine smile rather than a smirk.

I could kick myself now for letting him talk to me in the first place, to say nothing of the way my heart threatened to explode in happiness at the speech he gave me. "Listen. It's almost graduation, and I wouldn't feel right leaving this place if I didn't apologize for what an idiot I've been. Can you ever forgive me for acting like such a douchebag?"

At the time, it was the happiest moment of my life. I'm so sorry for that version of me who wanted so desperately to be liked. Of course, I accepted his apology, and when he asked if I wanted to dance, I just about floated up to the ceiling.

I still remember it so clearly—I can't even remember the last time I'd thought about that night, but it all comes back like it was yesterday. Like the memories have been waiting for me to return to them all these years. The song that was playing, sweet and gentle and a little swoony. Feeling so proud when I noticed everybody looking at us as Sawyer led me out onto the dance floor. The way his much larger hand engulfed mine, and how nice that felt. I was queen of the dance, at least in my wounded heart. I was getting my happy ending.

And that's what I believed right up until the moment we stopped dead in the center of the floor and Sawyer pushed me away from him, laughing. I didn't understand at first, thinking we were laughing together at how strange it was for the two of us, out of everybody in the school, to end up together on the dance floor.

My laughter didn't last long.

"She really thinks I want to dance with her!" he shouted to his asshole friends standing around the edges of the floor, watching us closely. "Can you believe this loser?"

Desperate. Deluded. I hear them in my head now, the way the words rang out that night. It seemed to come from all around me, everywhere I turned. Everybody was in on it, or so it felt at the time. Pointing, laughing, while Sawyer made a point of holding his arms out to his sides and puffing out his cheeks while he waddled ungracefully.

"Look at that dress!" he finally shouted, cackling, and all those cruel, stupid people joined in. Even some of the girls laughed—they wore sleek, sophisticated dresses that were probably a little too low-cut for kids our age. None of them wanted to look like a princess. They all wanted to be supermodels. I was a joke to them, too.

And looking back, I *was* desperate. Insanely desperate for acceptance and friendship. I'd spent my entire time at that school treated like an outsider, somebody who would never be one of them no matter where I went to college.

Look at you now. The voice in my head makes a good point. I can't pretend I haven't thought about those people from time to time as Sarah and I have built our business. Every so often, I'll remember the way it felt when I first started at the academy. Finding out there was no such thing as earning entrance to a rarefied world full of kids who only thought they were hot shit because they happened to be lucky enough to be born who they were, where they were, to whom they were. It had nothing to do with anything they'd earned—at least in my case, I'd earned the right to be there through hard work.

That didn't matter—if anything, they looked down on anybody who took their studies seriously the way I did. The term *scholarship student* was an insult. At least, that's how it always seemed to me, teased mercilessly, called a bookworm and all other kinds of much more hurtful names.

And now Sawyer needs me. The ringleader, the one person who could have brought it all to an end simply by telling everybody to lay off me. He had that kind of pull, that clout, the son of a billionaire whose money basically kept the school in business.

Sawyer made his choices. Considering he's in desperate need of my help, he hasn't changed much. Still running his mouth, still thinking he's God's gift. Nobody's as smart as he is, as clever as he is.

He's about to learn his lesson the hard way, and I can't wait to be the one to teach him.

Never go out of your way to make somebody miserable, because there might come a time when you need them badly. So badly, you're willing to offer nearly a quarter of a million to get you out of a jam you caused.

And even then, it won't be enough. Sawyer Cargill might be able to buy whatever his heart desires, but he can't buy forgiveness. He can't buy me.

7

SAWYER

"Have you heard anything yet?" I demand of my assistant as soon as she picks up her phone.

"No, Mr. Cargill." Theresa's soft, gentle voice is normally a comforting aspect of my job. I kept her on after Dad stepped down, both because it would have felt unfair to let her go over a situation she couldn't control, and because I could appreciate the value of a skilled, experienced employee when—let's face it—I didn't know the first thing about being a CEO. It's one thing to observe someone for years, but something completely different to take on the job yourself.

Now, she symbolizes every way in which I've fallen short. I'd bet she's sitting there right now reminding herself that my father would never be in this situation, taking a Saturday afternoon meeting due to an emergency he set in motion thanks to his wounded pride and big mouth.

"Let me know as soon as you get word she's arrived." I hang up before she can remind me we've already had this conversation, then get up from my desk and open the cleverly concealed door that sits flush against the wall. This is one of my favorite parts of the office, and when I was a kid it seemed like nothing less than magic to watch Dad press the panel and reveal a hidden room.

Of course, there was never anything inherently magical about it. Then, like now, the space was used as a dressing room complete with a small bed in case work runs too late. There are times when my schedule is too jammed to afford time to go home to change, much less to drag myself back to the apartment to sleep.

Now, I check out my reflection in the mirror mounted on the inside of the door. Everything's in place, my best Armani suit, its deep gray set off by a navy tie and crisp, white shirt. My shoes are polished to a mirror shine, and my dark hair is perfectly in place, swept back from my forehead without an errant strand in sight.

As a second thought, I duck into my private bathroom and grab the electric razor from the vanity. Sure, I shaved this morning, but I don't want so much as a hint of shadow on my cheeks. A quick pass with the device leaves me perfectly smooth. The man staring back at me in the mirror over the sink is one with the world at his feet and a bright future ahead of him.

He is certainly not shaking inside at the thought of the meeting going south.

I'm not thinking rationally. Everything's going to be fine. If Willow was able to take a last-minute meeting, she can't be too busy to take me on as a client. There's nothing about my situation so difficult she can't handle it—no tawdry twists, no thwarted girlfriends looking for revenge. No ex-employees I made the mistake of harassing. It should be a cut-and-dried job.

My nerves are jangling just the same. I can't leave anything to chance, because nothing has ever mattered this much.

Normally, in a situation such as this, I might let pride get in the way. I might warn myself against showing my entire hand all at once, leaving myself at this woman's mercy.

This is not a normal situation. I am entirely at her mercy, and I'm fine with her knowing that. Whatever it takes, so long as she gets me out of this. Even sweet, motherly Theresa couldn't hide a look of disapproval when she came in this morning at my request. This isn't the first weekend she's ever had to work, so I doubt her expression had anything to do with coming in on a Saturday.

Still, that's a walk in the park compared to the raft of shit handed to me by my brother Brooks once I finally gave in and answered his call. It's not often he has the opportunity to hold something over my head since I've managed to keep my nose pretty clean compared to his rampant womanizing. You can't swing a dead cat in this town without hitting a woman he hooked up with and discarded like a used tissue.

He made me regret giving him shit over that in the past during the twenty minutes he ranted and raved. "I'm not trying to step up and be CEO," he reminded me more than once. "I need you to get your shit together before you ruin my life along with yours." Working as our events manager is more than enough for him, I guess, giving him the opportunity to meet and socialize with countless women looking to throw bridal showers and birthday parties at the club without the added complication of stress and responsibility.

His verbal takedown echoes in my head as I take a seat behind my desk once again, straightening what's already been straightened. The rest of the office gleams thanks to the instructions I gave to the cleaning crew. They always do a good job, but I wanted special treatment for today. The dark wood floors seem to glow, and there isn't so much as a speck of dust on the leather furniture or along the frames of the art hanging on the walls. I didn't see any need to do much redecoration when I took over this office—Dad has always shown good taste when it comes to decor, and money was no object when he first began claiming this room as his own. Everything about it fairly screams sophistication, a discerning sense of taste.

Turning in my chair, even I have to admire the familiar but no less awe-inspiring view of the harbor. It's a stunning day, the sky a deep shade of azure without so much as a cloud to mar its beauty. Brilliant sunshine makes the water sparkle as if millions of diamonds were strewn across its surface. It's like Mother Nature herself is on my side, helping me create an image of wealth, grandeur. Everything about the club screams old money, precisely the way we want it to. Image is everything, after all, and I want this Willow Anderson to know who she's dealing with from the jump.

Anyone who walked in here right now and found me seated behind this old desk might think I was running for office. I'm the very image of the sort of guy people around here would vote for as their next governor; groomed within an inch of my life, with all the right names on my resume. The prestigious boarding school, the Ivy League university. I can't pretend the idea of going into politics never occurred to me before Dad announced I'd be taking his place, but that would mean taking time away from the family business.

When push comes to shove, this is what I want to do. I want to be here. I want to put my time, energy, my blood, sweat, and tears, if it comes to it, into this club. Not only to prove myself, either, but to maintain something real for my family. For the next generation, even if at the moment there's no such thing in sight. But there's still time. Maybe one day, I'll get to a place where I can think about settling down. Considering I'm fighting for my life at the moment, that's about as far from my mind as anything could be.

Everything is perfectly in place, but I'm too fidgety, too anxious to sit still. It's useless to try to get any work done, since all of my attention is focused on Willow's arrival. What will she be like? For a public relations expert, she has a very limited online presence. I would expect her to be all over social media, but then I can understand why she might want to fly under the radar. She probably knows all too well how easy it is to ruin yourself through a simple slip of the tongue—or of the fingers, as it were. I'm sure she's seen it all in her line of work and would rather bow out than take a chance.

Though I could tell her you don't have to be active on social media to end up crushed in its jaws.

What is taking her so long? I should have insisted she accept my offer of the helicopter, but she told me she was happy to make the drive. Every minute is another minute my reputation, my business, and my future hang in the balance. I can imagine Nathan and the rest of them lurking in the shadows, enjoying my humiliation even as they pretend to be mortified and concerned for me and the club.

Really, I'm sure they hope there's no coming back from this. It would make the process of getting rid of me go that much smoother. After all, Dad can only stick up for me through so much before even he won't be able to come up with a reason why they shouldn't kick me to the curb.

I wanted my phone to ring, didn't I? Yet for some reason, when it does, my stomach lurches and I wish I had more time. No matter who Willow has seen before today, I doubt she's ever met a client with so much on the line. So much so that I both long for and dread this meeting.

Get it together. I pick up the receiver. "Yes?"

"Sawyer, I just got the call from downstairs. She's on her way up." Even Theresa, always so collected, lets a note of anxiety leak into her voice. We don't have to discuss the situation in specifics for her to understand what's at stake. I'd like to think she's on my side, one of the few people who are.

"Thank you." My hand trembles ever so slightly as I replace the receiver, but I manage to make it stop before drawing a deep breath and releasing it slowly.

This is it. Everything rides on this.

All that's left is convincing Willow to do what she does best.

Otherwise, I might as well kiss this office, and the view, and everything that goes along with it goodbye forever.

8

WILLOW

Well. I have to admit, this is impressive.

Pulling up to the club, it's easy to understand how Sawyer got to be the way he is. I guess if you were raised in this world, you tend to adopt the idea that you're a big deal. The gorgeous, gleaming clubhouse shines like a beacon in the bright midday sun, promising wealth and exclusivity. I'm sure if anyone doubts for a moment just how special and privileged they are, they only need to pay a visit to the Yacht Club to be reminded.

Here, there's no chance of crossing paths with lesser humans—that is, except for the staff, but then I'm sure they don't count.

Alright, so I'm a little bitter. More than a little, in fact. Even though I'm rolling down the winding driveway in a Lexus, wearing a Chanel suit and carrying a Versace tote, I'm not fooling myself. Not like I did when I was a kid. I will never be one of them. I am merely a means to an end, another member of the staff. It doesn't matter how many zeroes there are in my fee. I'll never be on Sawyer's level.

That's fine by me. I've spent enough time around rich people to know I don't have much patience for them, anyway. It's sort of like the best of both worlds. I have plenty of money—not billions like the Cargill family, but I'm doing very well for myself. Still, I'm grounded. Realistic. I think that's what helps me with my job, being realistic. Understanding the way so-called common folk think. It's sort of my secret weapon, and it's invaluable.

When I look at it that way, the time I spent feeling undervalued and unwanted was a good thing, but I'll be damned if I thank Sawyer for it, though.

There's a valet waiting by the time I pull up to the big, circular courtyard at the entrance to the clubhouse. As soon as I open the door he extends a hand to help me from the car. "Good afternoon. Welcome to Somerset Harbor Yacht Club."

Boy, he has these kids trained well. I'm sure this is an excellent job for someone in their teens, though I've known enough wealthy people to doubt the tips are all that great. For the most part, the wealthy like to hold on to their wealth.

With that in mind, I slip the kid a fifty-dollar bill. "And you'll get another one when I come back," I promise, grinning to myself at the way his eyes light up. Something tells me he is going to baby my car.

Rather than go straight inside, I choose instead to take a short tour of the exterior. I want to get an idea what this place is like. What's at stake. Sure, he'll make it sound like the world is ending—and I'm sure for him, it feels like it is. I've found it's better to form my own opinion.

It's clear the staff takes pride in what they do. The grounds are manicured within an inch of their life. No matter how closely I look, I can't find so much as a blade of grass longer than the others. I can't help but imagine a gardener out here on his hands and knees, trimming with a pair of scissors to make sure nothing is missed. There's not a hint of a weed in the lush flower beds whose fragrance stirs a smile when a soft breeze carries it my way.

The sprawling building features a wide, deep terrace which I stroll across while gazing out at the harbor. It's like something out of a fantasy, some idealized image that could have come straight from a tourism ad. There are sailboats docked, bobbing gently on water that sparkles in the sun. My attention is focused in that direction while I round the building, eventually reaching an outdoor dining area overlooking the harbor.

On such a warm, brilliant day, I would expect every table to be full. Instead, they're at half capacity. I can't help but imagine how it must stick in Sawyer's craw to see this.

And I can't help smiling to myself. I'm sure he considers my arrival his salvation.

Is he in for a big surprise.

"Good afternoon." A pretty, bubbly girl wearing a sky blue polo approaches while I survey the dining area. "Will you be joining us for lunch today?"

"No, I'm here on business." Is it just me, or does her face fall slightly? Looking at her, I can't help but feel sorry for being pleased at how quiet things seem. I'm sure having fewer customers cuts into her tips, poor kid.

"I don't think there are any meetings scheduled for today, but I can go inside and check."

"I have a meeting with Mr. Cargill," I inform her with a gentle smile. "I was only taking a short walk around to explore before heading up."

"I see. Well, enjoy. If you need any assistance finding Mr. Cargill's office, just let me know." She hurries off to one of the tables and I continue my tour, heading back the way I came from. I almost wish I hadn't met that girl, because now I can't help thinking about all the other people whose livelihoods are at stake. If I were to take this job—which I am not going to do, not under any circumstances—I would do it for them, not for Sawyer.

If anything, my bitterness toward him only intensifies. It's not enough for him to screw up his own life. He has to jeopardize everybody around him, too. It doesn't come as a surprise, though. No matter how much time has passed, he is always going to be the person I knew back in the day. A leopard doesn't change its spots.

Our meeting was supposed to start five minutes ago, so I'm sure he's biting his nails down to the quick by now. The sudden lurch in my stomach speaks the truth I didn't want to admit to myself but can't avoid, I'm not only taking my time to make him sweat. When I get right down to it, I'm not looking forward to seeing him. Even though I know I'll have the upper hand, that he needs me way more than I ever needed him or ever will for that matter, the idea of being in the same room with him after all these years makes my palms sweat and my knees shake.

You can do this. One step at a time. I am not that girl anymore. I will not let him make me feel small or unworthy the way it was so easy for him to do when we were kids.

For the first time in his privileged life, Sawyer Cargill will be the one feeling small and unworthy.

I hope he can handle it.

But something tells me he can't.

9

SAWYER

If the entire universe conspired to drive me out of my skull, it succeeded. Never have I been so close to exploding, my blood pressure dangerously high, my nerves strained to the point of shredding. I have to keep my hands folded on the desk or else risk using them to throw something through the window.

Ten minutes. It has been ten minutes since she arrived, five minutes since our meeting was scheduled to start. I'm roughly two seconds away from bursting out of my office and marching downstairs to find the girl myself when there's a gentle tap against my door.

It opens slightly, with Theresa poking her graying head into the room. "Mr. Cargill? Miss Anderson is here for you."

I offer a brief smile meant to reassure her. "Thank you, Theresa." Straightening my tie, I stand, my heart in my throat. This is it. I need to be at my best, my most charming, my most personable. Considering my level of anxiety, it'll be a miracle on par with the parting of the Red Sea.

The door opens wider and Theresa ushers Willow inside.

I don't know what I was expecting. A polished, professional businesswoman, certainly. Considering she didn't express surprise or in fact any reaction at all to my offer of two hundred grand tells me she's no stranger to large fees.

What I didn't expect, what I couldn't possibly have expected, is how absolutely stunning she is. Instantly, the sight of her brings a smile to my face which I quickly temper into something more friendly and less... horny.

"Mr. Cargill." Her sweet, slightly husky voice does things to me most women haven't been able to do with both hands. She crosses the room, moving with grace, her heels tapping against the floor before she extends a hand. "I'm Willow Anderson."

I can't help but note how small her hand is, how slender her fingers. But then she's slender from head to toe, except where it counts. Her bust and hips are just big enough to give her an hourglass shape accentuated by what's clearly an expensive suit.

All of that passes through my head in a flash before my attention can focus on her brilliant, hazel eyes. You can tell a lot about a person by their eyes, and hers radiate intelligence when they meet mine. The corners of her full, glossy lips tick upward as we shake hands, and soon I realize why. I haven't said a word yet.

"Ms. Anderson," I finally manage to choke out. "Thank you so much for meeting with me, especially on a weekend."

"And especially last minute," she adds, punctuating her statement with a gentle laugh that for some reason leaves me twitching in my shorts. Oh, this is unfortunate. The woman holds my future in her hands, and all I can think about is getting her out of that suit and across my desk.

At this rate, I'll be lucky if she doesn't run out of here screaming harassment. Like I need things to get any worse.

Get it together. She's not the only attractive woman you've ever met. I'm sure there are half a dozen gorgeous, sexy women capable of holding a conversation in the dining room at this very moment. This woman is not unique.

“I'm sure it doesn't hurt that I'm more than willing to pay for the inconvenience. Please, have a seat.” I gesture toward the leather chairs positioned opposite my own. She perches gracefully, crossing her legs—smooth, lean, practically begging to be touched.

When was the last time I got laid? Clearly, it's been too long if I can't control my thoughts. All it takes is a flash of kneecap and I’m panting like a wolf in one of those old cartoons.

“Did Theresa offer you anything to drink? Maybe you'd like something from downstairs in the dining room.”

“No, thank you. I'm just fine.” There's something almost humorous in her voice, or maybe it's the Mona Lisa smile she wears. I can't quite tell what's going on in her head.

She sweeps lustrous, dark waves over her shoulder before folding her hands in her lap. “What can I do for you, Mr. Cargill? You didn't get into specifics in your emails.”

What can she do for me? What a loaded question. I can think of a lot of things I’d like from her, and none of them have anything to do with public relations.

"Putting it mildly, I screwed up. I was frustrated after an unsuccessful meeting with the town's officials. I'm in the process of getting approval to expand our dining room. It would mean building an addition onto the current structure, and there is a lot of red tape involved." She only murmurs in understanding, but doesn't say a word.

"Anyway, I was having a drink down at the bar with a friend of mine, and after a couple of whiskeys, my tongue got a little loose. I started to complain out of frustration. I insulted quite a few people—not by name," I'm quick to add in case she has any questions about that. "But in general. Little did I know, someone was recording every word."

"Cell phones can make venting in public a tricky thing."

"That's putting it mildly," I agree with a grimace. "As you can imagine, it's a nightmare. The video started to spread on social media, people got wind of it, the board is furious with me. I need to make things right."

She nods slowly, and nothing about her expression gives away what she's thinking. "I'm sure this can't be the worst thing you've ever dealt with," I point out, offering a sheepish grin.

"Not even close," she agrees with a soft chuckle. "But to you, I'm sure, it feels like the world is ending."

"You're not far from the truth," I admit, because what's the point of pride? I won't gain anything by trying to save face in front of her, even if the idea of admitting what an idiot I am in front of a beautiful woman leaves me gritting my teeth in discomfort. I need to remember this isn't just any gorgeous woman. And I can't afford to be distracted by the unfortunate fact of her beauty.

"Which platforms has the video been shared on?"

"Twitter and Facebook, mostly. And really, it's not like it went viral or anything, but it doesn't need to. All it took was a few shares with the right—or wrong—people for word to spread that I look down on everybody in town."

"Do you?"

The abruptness of her question damn near takes my breath away. I blink rapidly, waiting for her to laugh, but that unreadable smile remains in place. "Of course not. I was drunk, I was frustrated."

"That would explain the empty tables on your patio."

There's nothing inherently antagonistic about the way she says it—her voice is light, her tone frank and factual. She's only telling me what she observed for herself. Here I am, ready to argue what I know is true. That won't get me anywhere.

"Yes," I force myself to agree. "That would explain it. Before the video broke, we were so busy we had to turn people away on weekends."

"Hence the expansion plans."

"Exactly."

"Right now, it doesn't look like there's any need for you to expand. You might have solved your red tape problem without meaning to."

Again, my hackles rise, and now there's a telltale tightness in my chest. *Down, boy*. I can't afford to let pride get in the way. It was pride that got me into this mess in the first place. "That's where you come in," I remind her with a smile I don't completely feel. "If you're half as good as I've heard, you should be able to make this go away."

"I'm flattered," she murmurs, chuckling. "And please, don't misunderstand me. There's no judgment here. If it weren't for situations like this where people forget themselves and let their mouths run away from them, I wouldn't have a job."

So this is my fault? I practically have to bite my tongue off to contain that question, but I would very much like the answer. The way she makes it sound, I'm the one at fault. Like there was any way I could have known somebody was recording my every word. If anything, they're the ones to blame for infringing on my privacy.

"You mentioned your board earlier," she continues. "They're giving you a hard time?"

"You have no idea."

"How long have you been CEO of this place?"

"Longer than any of them believed I would manage," I admit, chuckling in spite of myself. "It's been less than a year."

"And do you make a habit of socializing here at the club?"

"I wouldn't say it's a habit," I point out. "There's something to be said for showing my face around here, though. Talking with the guests, letting the members know how valuable they are."

Her lips twist in a frown to go along with the drawing together of her brows. "It doesn't seem like you made them feel very appreciated, though."

This is her job. This is what she does. I need her. It would be a very, very bad idea to tell her exactly what I think about her opinions and observations. I might as well shoot myself directly in the foot if I let my temper get the better of me now.

"No, I didn't," I admit. Finally, I spread my arms in a shrug, palms up in a gesture of helpless surrender that doesn't come easily to me. "I've laid myself bare for you, Ms. Anderson. I'm willing to accept the fact that my pride got in the way and left me in this mess. All I need to know now is, how do we make it better?"

"We?" A soft smile punctuates the question. "Remember, Mr. Cargill, we aren't officially working together."

Yet. I wait for her to add the word *yet*, but she doesn't.

Something very close to dread begins to build in my gut, growing like a balloon with every silent moment that passes between us. Finally, I have to ask, "And what will it take for us to make it official? Money is no object, Ms. Anderson. If I haven't offered enough, if you think this will take more work than usual, by all means. Name your price, and consider it paid. This is my future we're talking about. My professional reputation, my reputation here in town. I have to live around these people, don't forget. I need to make it right."

"What ever happened to issuing an apology and promising to do better? Speaking frankly, it isn't like you run some big, international corporation. I'm sure Somerset Harbor feels like the entire world when you live here, but really, you're a big fish in a very small pond. You might have to eat crow for a little while, but I have no doubt this will all fade away in time."

She leans forward, her eyes gleaming with intense interest that verges on the unnerving. "Why is it so important that we fix this right away? Why are you willing to spend so much money, in other words?"

I force a tight laugh. "I've never met anyone who would question a fee like the one I'm offering."

"I need to know the full story if there's any hope of helping you, which means I need to understand the stakes. What is truly at stake for you? What is your end goal?"

At first, my tongue feels too thick to speak. This is the one thing I didn't want to have to say out loud —and the fact that she seems to stare straight through me with those brilliant hazel eyes of hers isn't helping. She makes me want to hide, an impulse I can't make heads or tails off.

“Fine,” I relent. “You want to rake me over the coals?” Her brows draw together, but she says nothing. “I need to make this go away before my father hears about it.”

Her lips twitch. “See? Now we're getting down to the truth. You're afraid he'll take the job away?”

“Among other things. Come on, don't tell me you can't relate to the situation. I don't want to disappoint my father. Even a grown adult feels that way sometimes, don’t they?”

“Yes, that's a good point. But again, in the spirit of honesty, he would unseat you if the board told him to, wouldn't he?”

The thought makes my skin feel like it’s too tight, like I’m going to burst out of it. A cold sweat begins to bead on the back of my neck. “I would hope not, but honestly? I can't tell. He is completely unreachable, on vacation in the Virgin Islands. But there's only so much he can do to dissuade the board—and once they vote, there's nothing he can do about it. So you see my position.”

"At last," she finally murmurs, nodding slowly. "Now I see the full situation."

She sighs softly, her lips pressing into a thin line. *Come on, Willow. Tell me what I want to hear.* Honestly, if I didn't know any better, I would think she was busting my balls on purpose. Like she's enjoying herself, like there's something funny about any of this.

It's almost enough to make me wonder if we've met before, but that's not possible. I would remember her. I've had my share of women, but I don't forget anyone as stunning as she is, not to mention as intelligent and unafraid to break my balls a little. She is nothing if not memorable. Yet she looks at me like she's seen me before—and she's unimpressed.

She sighs again, this time sitting up a little straighter, and I hold my breath in anticipation. "First things first," she begins, arching an eyebrow. "I would recommend banning all recording devices in the club from this day forward."

"Oh." I didn't expect that. "That's a big ask. Everyone carries a phone."

"Still, you can insist phones either be left outside, or at least unused when your guests are within these walls. It's easily enforceable, really. One of your staff sees somebody on their phone and all they have to do is gently remind them of the new policy."

"Alright. I see your point." Besides, most of our members are at an age where they aren't glued to their devices nearly as much as people of my generation. If anything, our new policy will hit the staff the hardest, but they shouldn't be screwing around on their phones during work hours, anyway.

"And that," Willow continues, reaching for the tote bag beside her chair, "you can consider a little free advice. I won't even charge you for it."

My stomach sinks when she rises. "That's it?"

"That's it," she confirms. "Otherwise, I would recommend you fuck off. You're out of your mind if you think I will ever lift a finger to help you."

"Excuse me?" I push the chair back from the desk in shock, staring at her with my mouth hanging open while my heart thuds against my ribs like a bass drum.

"That wasn't clear enough for you?" Now she smiles like a shark, her eyes going hard and cold. "I'll make it clearer. No, Mr. Sawyer Cargill, I will not be accepting your offer. I would rather eat glass than lift a finger to help you fix the mess you got yourself into. But good luck."

Turning on her heel, she marches to the door. "You're going to need it," she calls out over her shoulder before striding smoothly out into the hall.

And all I can do is watch her go, stunned into frozen silence at the sight of my last hope walking away from me.

10

WILLOW

Are there trumpets blaring as I leave his office, or are they only in my head? It takes every scrap of my self-control not to look over my shoulder and savor more of his open-mouthed horror, but somehow I manage.

Now I know one thing for sure, he doesn't remember me. Then again, why would he? I don't look much like I did back then.

A fact which he certainly seemed to enjoy. It's almost enough to make bile rise in my throat, the memory of how he pretty much ogled me when I first walked into the room. Sure, now that I've lost weight and have the money to afford better clothes and a good haircut, I'm worth paying attention to. And worth noticing, worth being kind to.

And of course, I can help him get away with this before Daddy finds out. I knew his father had to be at the heart of everything. He can't disappoint Daddy. What a child.

Maybe now he'll think twice before he shoots his mouth off. Telling me he doesn't really look down on the people living in town. I'm surprised I was able to keep a straight face. Sarah will be proud.

Though I might forget to mention the part where I told him to fuck off. And maybe where I said I'd rather eat glass.

"Come on, come on," I whisper, jamming my finger against the elevator button a second time. The damn thing is so slow. It's going to ruin my moment of triumph. What's the good of getting the last word in if you give your opponent enough time to recover and come up with a crushing response?

"Ms. Anderson!"

Shoot! My eyes dart around as panic blooms in my chest. I was so close to getting away. I don't have the first idea where the stairwell is, or else I'd be running down to the ground floor right this very second.

His heavy tread rings in my ears and the elevator is still nowhere near arriving, so there's nothing left to do but lift my chin and face him as he storms out of his office. Even now, I can't help but admit to myself what an impressive image he creates, his muscular body perfectly encased in a gorgeous, tailored suit that fits him like a glove.

"Exactly what the hell is going on?" he demands when he finds me standing in the hall. "Here I was, thinking you were a professional, when you're anything but."

"I'm sorry to disappoint you," I mutter. "Though considering the fact it was you who got caught shooting his mouth off in his place of business, I'd say the pot's calling the kettle black."

He comes to a stop a few feet away from me, folding his arms before looking me up and down. He's not checking me out anymore, not the way he was before. Maybe he finally realizes I'm more than a pair of boobs attached to a body.

"What have I done to offend you?"

"Who says you did anything?"

"Give it a break," he retorts. "You don't tell somebody you'd rather eat glass than work with them if there's not something personal underneath it. So what is it? What did I do to deserve that? I came to you in good faith, assured you were the best. I answered your questions, as rude as they were. What else do you want from me?"

This is too delicious. Now I wish Sarah had come with me so she could watch him fall to pieces, and all because somebody told him no. "You aren't used to being refused, are you?" I ask, tipping my head to the side. His cheeks go dark, telling me I hit a nerve.

"There you go again," he growls, and the sound is enough to make the hair on the back of my neck rise. "Getting personal. Why don't you do me a favor and clue me in? Say what you want about me, but I at least like to know my opponent. And right now, you seem to have me at a disadvantage."

"You really don't remember me?" I whisper, grinning. "Honestly? I don't ring a bell at all?"

His head snaps back, his eyes going narrow, and there's practically smoke coming out of his ears as he tries to figure it out. I have nowhere better to be, so I wait, still grinning while he struggles.

Finally, he throws his hands into the air. "No. I don't remember you."

As if on cue, the elevator chimes softly and the doors slide apart. I step inside the car, turning to face him while pushing the button for the ground floor. "Think about it." The doors slide shut, separating us.

And now I can sigh in relief, my muscles loosening, my heart racing. Only now it's racing from joy, victory. I did it. I finally did it. Maybe he'll never put two and two together, but I will know I made him pay for all the indignities he put me through, for the cruelty I never did anything to deserve. All it took was my existence for him to torment me.

Now the shoe is on the other foot, and I have to bite my lip to hold back a giggle of sheer giddy relief. The theme from the *Rocky* movies rings out in my head, and I can't wait to tell Sarah every last detail of how I finally humiliated Sawyer Cargill. I might have to jump up and down with my fists in the air while I do so.

I can imagine every fist pump—that is, until the doors open and I come face to face with him once again. Only this time, he's out of breath. "You're not getting away from me that easy," he pants. Did he run down the stairs? He really is desperate.

"I have no time for this," I inform him with a shrug. "My answer was final. Now if you will excuse me..." I try to step around him on exiting the elevator, but he's too damn stubborn to let me get by.

"I have no idea who you are," he insists, placing his body between me and the door. "But you must hate me if you came all the way out here just to say no. Why? What did I ever do to you? What could be worth it?"

"You want to know why I would come all this way just to turn you down?" I mimic his posture, folding my arms and wishing I were just a little taller. Even in four-inch heels, he's got half a foot on me. I'd rather not have to look up to him.

"I think that's the least you can tell me after your rudeness."

"Oh, was I rude?" I touch a hand to my chest, batting my eyes. "Forgive me. I wouldn't want to be rude. I bet that made you feel pretty small and helpless, didn't it?"

"Don't put words in my mouth."

"But it did. I can tell it did, or else you wouldn't have run all the way down here."

"This has nothing to do with that. This is important to me. I need this to go away."

"Newsflash, it's not going away. No matter what happens, you'd have to put in the hard work of making up for the stupid things you said. But I understand how you'd be uncomfortable with that since that's not exactly something you've had to do much of."

"Damn it," he mutters. "Why? Why are you doing this? Why go to all this trouble?"

"I guess I want to watch you grovel," I admit, lifting a shoulder.

The man has the nerve to scoff. "I wouldn't say I groveled."

"Even now," I marvel, shaking my head. "Even now, you can't help but let your stupid pride get in the way."

"Is that what you want? For me to grovel?"

Glancing around him, I notice an older couple on their way inside the building. "Careful," I whisper. "You don't want to dig your grave any deeper by embarrassing yourself in front of your guests."

"You are unbelievable," he whispers.

Am I? Or am I only one of many people who have wanted nothing more than a little bit of help or kindness from him over the years? Am I merely denying him what he refused to give others time and again?

"So you say," I murmur with a shrug. "And maybe I am. But I promise, if you give it a little more thought, you might finally figure out why I came here and what this is all about."

"I don't particularly care to figure out why you have a vendetta against me," he fires back. "All I want is your help."

"You can't be serious."

"Do I look like I'm joking? I told you what's at stake. I told you what I need. How important this is."

"There are other—"

"I don't have the time to find anyone else," he's quick to insist. "I put all my eggs in this basket. I need you. I need the best."

I'd be lying to myself if I pretended this isn't even slightly gratifying. Hearing him say he needs me. I mean, he's right. He needs me big time.

Still... "You wouldn't listen to a single thing I said, so what's the point? It would be a waste of time."

"Once again, you're standing here acting like you know me, and you won't even tell me how. For all I know, you're making it up."

"I am not," I whisper, gritting my teeth. "I promise."

"Then tell me who you are! Whatever I did, I was wrong. And I'm sorry. Whatever you need to hear."

"You honestly think it's that easy?"

"Why does it have to be more difficult?" he counters. Again, he has to lower his voice when a group of guests passes by, and I have the benefit of watching them roll their eyes and nudge each other at the sight of him.

"Spoken like someone who has never been the victim of somebody like you."

"Victim? When did I ever victimize you? Would you get to the point already and tell me what is so damn important that you would be willing to throw away the kind of money I'm willing to pay?"

"Yes, there it is. Right on schedule." I'm almost disappointed in him.

"Exactly what does that mean?"

"Money," I tell him, sounding it out slowly. "You think that's all it takes. Throw enough money at a problem, and it goes away. I figured you hadn't changed, and now you've confirmed it. You grew up in this world." I wave a hand, indicating everything around us. "And you think your money can get you out of anything. Surprise, Mr. Cargill. There are situations even your vast fortune can't get you out of. Because at the end of the day, there is no amount of money in this world enough to make up for a person's bad behavior. Not really. Not when it counts. Not right now. Have you ever heard of karma?"

"No," he replies, rolling his eyes, his voice dripping with sarcasm.

"Well, today is the day it catches up with you. I'm just happy I could be here for it."

This time, when I walk around him, he doesn't stop me. The door is only a few yards ahead, and I find myself almost running for it. I need to get away from him. I need this to be over.

"What if I double the offer?" he calls out behind me, freezing me in place at his audacity. "I don't want to argue anymore, and I don't really care who you are, but I need your help. What do you say?"

What do I say?

I say I really wish I could've gotten out of here with the last word.

11

SAWYER

I am absolutely baffled by this woman. Completely out to sea, with no hope of understanding the effect she has on me.

She's insulted me. Walked away from me. Even taunted me with a depth of bitterness that makes this feel personal. She hates me for some reason, that much is obvious. And she isn't afraid to rub my face in it.

Considering all of this, the last thing I should want to do is throw her to the floor and fuck her senseless. Yet here I am, knocked sideways by the force of my attraction. She is so damn fuckable, from head to toe. Every part of her tempts me in some way; thick, shining hair begging for my hands to sink in deep before pulling her close. Pouty lips whose taste I'd love to memorize, who's firmness I'd love to test. And what my hands couldn't do to her body.

She hates me, she wants to humiliate me, and I'm still fighting off an erection. I'm not sure what this says about me, and I'm not sure I like it. I only know there's no denying it.

"I'm waiting for an answer," I murmur. Of all places for us to do this, but then I'm not the one who tried to leave without really settling things. She seems to know me, yes, but she can't know me very well if she honestly believed I would accept her rejection without doing everything in my power to change her mind.

"You've already gotten your answer." She lifts her head before spinning on her heel and pinning me to the spot with a glare that could melt steel. Beautiful eyes, clear and sparkling, but now they burn with resentment. Nothing has ever been more important than finding out why. What did I do? How do I make it right?

I'm not even sure I care more about the business or our personal involvement anymore. Yes, I need her, but the lines are blurred thanks to what boils down to unprofessionalism on her part and what feels like masochism on mine.

"You honestly think everybody has a price, don't you? After everything I've already said, you're still doing your best to buy my help."

It got you to stop before you walked out the door, didn't it? Something tells me throwing that in her face would be the worst move I could make, so I bite my tongue. "I need this. What can I do to make you understand?"

"I understand very well."

"And you hate me enough to leave me hanging, even so?"

"Even so." She's so proud of herself, probably envisioning some grand, sweeping moment of triumph as she lifts her chin in defiance. "Sorry to burst your bubble, but there are still people who believe integrity means something."

"Do me a favor and let me know how the company who owns your office building would feel if you tried to use integrity to pay your rent."

"I'm doing just fine without your... generous offer." Her lips twitch with wry humor and it should make me want to tear her to pieces for mocking me, but all I want is to tear that tailored suit from her body and get familiar with every inch of her.

"But you could be doing much better. Let's stop kidding ourselves. I'm offering you nearly half a million dollars."

"Good for you."

"What else is it going to take?"

"You could offer me two million, and the answer would be the same. Why don't you stop wasting your time? Your time could be better spent searching for a representative who'd be happy to handle your problem."

"It has to be you." I don't know why and doubt I could pull my thoughts together if there were a gun to my head. Call it pride, call it stupidity. I will not let this woman walk away.

Her eyes dart around, taking in the expertly appointed lobby. "Then I hope you aren't too attached to any of this, because it won't be yours for much longer."

"What is it? Why won't you tell me what I did to deserve this?"

"Maybe it's fun watching you scramble around, trying to figure it out." She tips her head to the side, a shrewd expression settling over her delicate features. "Then again, no. You're not trying to figure it out. You want to bulldoze your way through this and twist everything to your liking, no matter what it means for me. That's a lot closer to the truth, isn't it?"

I'm about sick to death of the way she thinks she knows me—even if she is correct. If anything, that makes it worse. "Whatever I did, I'm sure I didn't mean it."

She lowers her brow, eyes blazing. "You meant it."

"How would you know? There are always two sides to a story."

"I'm sure that's what you tell yourself every time you run your mouth or conveniently forget other people have lives and dreams and goals."

Shit. No, I'm no closer to remembering this woman, but the way her voice trembles and almost cracks with emotion tells me this is even more serious than I suspected. It's the first hint she's given so far of real feeling.

"Listen." I hold out my hands, palms out, a gesture of surrender. "I really would like to know the full story, but this isn't the place to share it. Could you please come back up to my office where we will have a civil, adult conversation?"

"I have no desire—"

"You must, or else you wouldn't have come all this way. You insulted me, and maybe I deserve it, but the least you can do is tell me why. That's all I ask."

Lowering my brow the way she did, I add, "Unless you're such a chicken shit, you thought it would be enough to insult me and run away before I could get a word in."

"Don't call me that," she warns. "You are not going to goad me."

"Fair enough." I hold out an arm, gesturing to the elevator. "Please. I need to know what inspired all of this."

I might as well be a fox in the hen house judging by the way she looks me up and down. What could I have done to her to inspire this? I would remember a woman like her—granted, I've been through my fair share, but this girl is special. Did I overlook her somehow?

"Fine," she huffs. "But this is in no way to be mistaken for acceptance of your offer." With her arms folded, she stalks back to the elevator, tapping her foot while I push the button for service. It hasn't been used since she stepped out of it, so the doors slide open immediately, and she makes a big deal of marching into the car in front of me.

I need to get myself together, because being this close to her even in an innocent way has my dick lengthening. The faint scent of her perfume—light, floral, with a note of vanilla—is enough to unleash hunger deep inside me, a dangerous sort of hunger that might make me forget to behave myself.

She doesn't say a word until we're off the elevator and on our way down the hall again. "It shouldn't surprise me that you don't remember. I'm sure I was one of many."

"One of many what?" I demand once we're alone again. This time I close the door since I don't want Theresa or anybody else overhearing this. After all, I'm not sure what she has to say. Was it a drunken fling? Surely, this can't have anything to do with business. Our paths wouldn't have crossed in that way before now, at least as far as I know. I didn't recognize her name when Jayden gave it to me, either.

"One of many people you've humiliated and bullied through the years."

Bullied? "I don't make it my business to bully people."

"That's rich. Then again, maybe you've changed since then." She turns away from me, studying the room. "This is very nice. Classy, tasteful. It screams money, which I guess is the point."

I wish this didn't feel so much like a chess match, or maybe a tango. I don't know the steps. All I can do is scramble to keep up. "It was my father's office."

Her snort tells me what she thinks of this. "Of course it was. And now it's yours because you happened to be born to him." She goes to the row of bookshelves along the wall to the right of my desk. "Nice looking family," she observes in a soft voice while examining a photo of all of us together in front of the building in which we now stand.

"Enough observations on my family and my business. What did you mean by bullying? How did I bully you? Why don't we get down to the point?" As entertaining as it is, playing out this tango, we are wasting time. I can't lose sight of what's at stake.

Her shoulders rise and fall when she sighs deeply. "I guess I have changed a little. It's not surprising you wouldn't recognize me at first sight, and I'm sure you never bothered to learn my full name."

No, I suppose I didn't. I can't recall ever knowing someone by the name Willow. No matter how I search my memory, desperate to catch up to her.

She turns to face me, and now her eyes are flat and cold. There might even be a touch of sadness in them. "I don't suppose you ever thought you'd be offering this spotty, chubby kid with frizzy hair and thick glasses the chance to save your ass, did you?"

Chubby? Frizzy hair? It's impossible to imagine that while staring at what's in front of me.

"When you humiliated me at the senior dance until I had no choice but to run away in tears, it never occurred to you that the day would come when you'd offer me hundreds of thousands of dollars to save you. Am I right, Sawyer?"

The senior dance. Christ, that feels like a lifetime ago. I haven't thought about it in years, probably not since graduation.

But now that she mentions it...

I back away, because now I need to sit down. Willow. The senior dance. A girl in a ridiculous, fluffy dress running away while everybody laughs at her. Because of me.

"No." I sink into my chair, but my heart continues sinking after I'm seated.

"Maybe I should have introduced myself using the name you gave me." Her heels click sharply against the floor as she closes in on me like a predator closing in on her prey. "I should have called myself Wallowing Willow. Maybe that would have jogged your memory."

Oh, fuck me. Now I get it. Now it all makes sense in the worst possible way. I want to dissolve into the floor, to dig a hole and never come out.

I can't look her in the eye now. "Willow..." I mumble, at a loss. Mortification squeezes my throat and threatens to choke the life out of me, while all she can do is snicker.

"You have no idea, do you? How you crushed me back then. And why? What did I ever do to you to deserve that?"

That's the thing. I have no idea what she did because she more than likely didn't do anything. "I was stupid."

"No kidding."

"And thoughtless, and cruel."

"I am not going to disagree with you."

Looking back, I honestly can't recall a moment when she did or said anything to set me off. She was... different. Exactly as she described herself, chubby, with a face full of acne and glasses that made her eyes look huge. The sleek, lustrous hair still tempting my fingers was a frizzy cloud back then.

But none of it is an excuse. There is no excuse to make up for what I did.

Her spine stiffens. "As you already know, I'm not that girl anymore. I doubt you would give me the time of day if I were."

"That's not true. Some of us actually grow up between the ages of seventeen and twenty-nine."

"Maybe so. I know I have. And now, I'm the woman who can clean up your image and fix everything for you—but I won't. No matter how much money you offer because you can't buy me. For once, you're going to suffer the consequences of your actions, both what you did back then, and the way you ran your mouth like an idiot in front of your club members."

I'm still stunned, but not so stunned that I don't notice the way she begins to back up. She's leaving, and this time, it's for good. She's finally had her say. Damn it, she deserves it. I made a mockery of her. I went out of my way to humiliate her.

"I'm sorry. Truly, truly sorry."

"Pardon me?" she murmurs, her eyebrows lifting so high I'm surprised they don't disappear into her hairline.

"What, you don't think I'm capable of apologizing when I'm in the wrong? And I was. I was very much in the wrong, and there's no excuse for it." The more I reflect, the worse my shame becomes. I mimicked her as cruelly as I could, and all because I wanted to get a laugh from a bunch of assholes who have played no part in my life since then.

"Yes, you were," she mutters. No wonder she's so guarded, with that enormous chip on her shoulder.

"I deeply regret what I did back then. Really, I do, and I'm glad you're here to remind me of it. I was an obnoxious asshole. Being young is not an excuse. I wish I could go back and change it, I truly do, because I'm ashamed of who I was. But there's no changing the past. I can only do everything in my power to make up for it."

"I never asked you to."

"No, but I want to."

"Believe me. This is repayment enough. Watching you squirm while everything you care about is on the line. Trust me, I'm getting more than enough satisfaction from that."

"Even when I've expressed regret? You're going to punish me for something I did more than a decade ago?"

Her blithe shrug gives me little hope. "Why not? You punished me for something I *never* did. Do you honestly think any of the boys we went to school with would have given me the time of day? No way. Even if they liked me, they wouldn't risk attracting attention from you or your asshole friends. It was too much of a risk. Those were the most miserable years of my life, and it was all thanks to you. Sorry to break it to you, Sawyer, but that's the kind of pain a person carries with them. I do understand you not having the first clue, because up until now, everything's been so easy for you."

She doesn't know me. She sees straight through me, beyond the image I've crafted for the public.

"I've changed. I've grown up."

All she does is snort derisively, her nose wrinkling like she smells something foul. "Go fuck yourself, Sawyer."

"Really, Willow? What else do I have to do? Get on my knees and beg? Offer to strip naked and jump in the harbor? Maybe you'd like it if I let you parade me around town on a leash like the dog I am. Would that make it better?"

"Careful," she murmurs, leaning closer from the other side of the desk and lessening the distance between us. "You're going to let your temper get the better of you, and we all know what happens when you do."

Damn it, she's right again.

"Ms. Anderson," I manage to murmur after taking a deep breath, "everything I have is on the line, and I am entirely open to whatever you have in mind to make things right. I will do everything you say, down to the letter. Please, I need your help. I'm sorry for everything I did—I'm ashamed of it, really I am. And I have never begged for anything in my life, but I am begging you now. Please, do this for me, and you'll get every penny I promised. I need you—your help," I quickly amend.

She straightens up, lips pursed, and I find myself cautiously optimistic. She hasn't thrown my words in my face or stormed out of the room yet. She's wavering, debating with herself.

"Let's face it," I add, daring to grin. "I'm giving you the opportunity to boss me around and get paid handsomely for it. That alone should be worth considering."

I can't believe I'm making a complete fool of myself for this woman, but what's at stake is much bigger than my pride. And I will do anything it takes to fix my mess.

Though I can't pretend the idea of working closely with the spitfire in front of me doesn't sweeten the deal a little. And if I can make things right between us, so much the better, because I hurt her.

It looks like there's much more at stake here than I could ever have anticipated.

All I need is for her to let go of her pride long enough to accept my offer.

12

WILLOW

This is ridiculous. I should be out of here, on my way home by now. Sarah and I should be planning where we'll meet up for our celebratory champagne. I finally had my say. I finally put him in his place. There's no question anymore of whether or not he remembers me. He does, and even though I wouldn't give him much credit otherwise, I can almost believe he's sorry. Not because of the way his bullying rippled down through the years and affected the here and now, but really, truly. I believe he's sorry for what he did.

In other words, this has gone better than I could have hoped. I should end on a high note and get out of here. I really should.

So why can't I? My feet are suddenly too heavy, rooted to the floor. Maybe it's his gaze that does it, that penetrating stare of his.

"This isn't a good idea." I wave a hand between the two of us. "You and me? I would hate to ruin all this nice furniture with the blood that's going to flow."

"It's insured."

To my dismay, I find myself fighting back a laugh at his deadpan response. He doesn't blink. His gaze doesn't waiver. "What do you say? Four hundred grand is a lot of money."

"Even for somebody like you?"

"Even for somebody like me."

What is wrong with me? Did I use up all of my outrage and indignation too soon? I must have because I'm weakening. I'm actually considering taking him up on this, and it disgusts me. Have I forgotten everything he did? Whatever happened to pride? Don't I have any left?

But my God, this is a lot of money we're talking about. And we could do a lot of things for the business with a sum that large. We could hire more staff, maybe even expand our office. The lease on the offices across the hall from ours will be up in a month or two, last I checked. We could take the entire floor, hire a few more associates. We might even be able to afford a little time off every once in a while instead of handling day-to-day operations ourselves.

"You mean to tell me you would be okay with being bossed around?"

His forehead creases in a brief but noticeable frown. "Yes?" I can't help but snicker, and he offers an affable grin. "I told you how important this is. I think I can learn to follow directions if it means getting out of this mess."

That's not exactly what I'm concerned with. "You mean to tell me your pride wouldn't get in the way? You've matured that much?"

"You didn't know me all that well back then."

"I knew as much as I needed to."

"My point is, I'm not who you think I am."

I can't even pretend to go along with that one. "I see. So deep down inside, you're just a simple guy with simple needs, is that it? A poor little rich boy who has no problem listening to people who know better than he does?"

"I wouldn't use those exact words, but you're pretty close."

"Then what was with the bitch session that got you into this mess in the first place?" The way he stammers makes me raise an eyebrow. "Nothing about what you've described gives me the impression of a humble, *Aww shucks* kind of guy."

"That was different."

"How so? Because from what you described, you were pissed off at having to go through the same red tape everybody else and their mother has to deal with. What makes you so special?"

"I was frustrated, damn it." His face is starting to go red and his voice is sharp and this is exactly what I expected to happen.

"Alright," I murmur. "You were frustrated. I can understand that. But you also managed to reveal your true feelings about the people in this town, whom you clearly think are beneath you. Correct?"

"Don't put words in my mouth."

Releasing a heavy sigh, he leans back in his chair, loosening his tie as he does. Good. He's dropping the act, no longer playing the part of the buttoned up businessmen. It doesn't suit him—the whole thing comes off as an act.

"I was drunk and I was frustrated and yeah, I guess I was feeling superior. And yes, it's because they were denying me what I needed. But don't make the mistake of thinking that's how I normally behave. I've never been anything but professional and gracious otherwise."

"Never?"

There's something satisfying about the way he squirms, and I have to hold back a smile. If I didn't know better, I would think I was flirting with him, but that's not going to happen. No matter how he thinks he's changed, the truth is in front of us. If he had really changed, he would not be in this situation. Deep down inside, there's still part of him that thinks he's better than everybody else. Maybe he doesn't know it, but it's there.

"I'm telling you, this was a one-off. What do you want to do? Break my balls a little more? Here, do you want to step on them?" He pushes back from the desk, legs spread, and unexpected heat rises in me.

I don't know what it is. Maybe the sight of his impressive body in that suit, or how sexy he looks in a disheveled kind of way—the loosened tie, the sprawled out posture. All I know for sure is there's heat rising, so intense it creeps up my neck and colors my cheeks.

"No, thank you," I manage while pulling the scraps of my self-respect together.

"I just need to know you're going to do this, and then we have to get started. This situation gets worse by the minute. I need you."

I need you. That, plus those dark, puppy dog eyes of his reveal something about me I didn't even know until now. I have secretly craved a situation like this all along. Knowing he needs me, being the one who holds his future in my hands. He needs me, or else everything falls apart. It's exciting, a thrill, and almost too satisfying.

There may or may not be a telltale buzzing between my thighs, and that's the most telling part of all. The way his begging excites me.

The way I can't help but wonder what else I could make him beg for.

Stop the train, change tracks, end this here. It's bad enough I'm entertaining the idea of accepting his offer. I don't need to add lust to the mix, no matter how insanely attractive he is.

Okay, more than attractive. He's hot as hell, just like he's always been.

I'm a grown woman, aren't I? I'm not that girl anymore, the one who was so easily wounded. I've got my shit together, and I have a business partner to account for, too. Giving up on that kind of fee would cut into Sarah's bottom line just as much as it would mine, and expanding our business would benefit her as much as it would me. How could I live with myself if I admitted to turning down four hundred grand, all because a boy was mean to me in high school?

Who are you trying to convince? If there's one thing about me, it's that I like to be honest with myself. That voice in the back of my head is what keeps me honest, and it is not buying a single one of my rationalizations. Sure, this represents a big opportunity, but there are plenty of opportunities out there. I don't need to sacrifice my pride for any amount of money.

At the heart of the matter is the way he draws me in. I should have left without another word, but somehow he convinced me to continue talking. Even after I've said everything that has weighed on me all these years, I'm still standing here. All because he wants me to. Because for some reason, he has that power.

That's what has me moving closer to accepting the offer. That's what's tempting me to stay when I should be miles away by now.

"Did you mean it when you said you would do everything I told you, down to the letter?"

His eyes light up as his head bobs up and down. "Every single thing. No arguments. I trust you."

"So your pride isn't going to get in the way?"

"All that matters is fixing this. There's no room for pride."

Okay, so that's a turn on. The idea of bossing him around some more, peeling back the layers of the pride he swears doesn't matter but I know secretly does. He would agree to anything right now. I bet I really could get him to strip down and jump in the harbor.

He's that desperate, and is only getting more desperate with every passing second. He can try to play it off all he wants, but he is not a good actor. He wants to pounce, to demand, and the only thing holding him back is knowing how quickly I would drop the whole thing if he did. He's a lot of things, but he isn't stupid. He may even have learned a thing or two about human nature in the years between high school and now.

He knows one false move will bring all of this to an end. He knows he's lucky I've stayed this long.

Poor, lonely, teenage Willow is jumping for joy inside me, clapping her hands, soaking up every last drop of his humiliation. But it's not enough to know he knows he screwed up. I'm going to make sure I pay him back every single day we work together. Pretty soon he's going to see exactly how much room there is for pride in a situation like this, because I'm going to chip it away from him a little bit at a time. And he'll have no choice but to suck it up, or else I'll leave him hanging.

"Okay."

Sawyer sits up straight, almost at the edge of his seat, his dark eyes darting over my face like he can't quite believe it. "Yes? You'll do it?"

"We'll have to go over the contract carefully, but I don't see any reason why we can't work together so long as you are willing to go along with everything I say, no questions asked."

"Done." He just about jumps out of his chair, extending a hand. "I'm completely under your control."

He needs to be careful saying things like that, or else I might not be able to contain my giddy excitement. This is better than leaving him hanging, I realize as I extend my hand to shake his. I can torture him slowly, override everything he wants, keep him guessing. For the first time in his life, he is not going to be the one calling the shots. I'll have the thrill of watching him subjugate himself to me—and if he doesn't want to, I'll have even more fun reminding him of what little choice he has.

I'll give him the best free branding any company has ever seen. The job I do with him will be a case study for all future clients.

And if it means finally getting the respect I craved all those years ago, so much the better.

By the time this is over, I'll be the one on top. And he will regret ever underestimating me.

"So." Lowering my bag to the floor, I take a seat. "Let's get started."

His face practically glows as he takes his seat again, and I'd swear he looks five years younger now that he's not so worried. "Great. I was thinking—"

"Hold on." Here he is, already trying to take the reins. I hold up a warning finger, wagging it back and forth. "Remember. You're letting me call the shots. Which means you don't get to boss me around and tell me what you think we need to handle first. I'm going to help you. I'm going to do a very good job of it. But I will be the one calling all the shots. Got it?"

His lips twitch in something close to a smile. "I can handle that."

Can he? I have my doubts.

For the first time in his privileged life, Sawyer Cargill has come up against a true adversary who isn't afraid to stand up to him.

No, I don't think he has the first idea what he's in for.

13

SAWYER

I did it. I actually did it. I got her to agree. The satisfaction that spreads through me when she pulls out her phone, already creating a list of tasks, her lips pursed in concentration... It's almost too much to handle while still remaining silent, composed. What I want is to run down the hall hooting and whooping and swinging my suit jacket around my head like a victory flag.

I have to remind myself this is only the first of many steps. I might have gotten her to come around and agree to help me, but I'm still no closer to solving this problem. Amazing how my priorities shifted so suddenly. That's the power she has, and it's almost intimidating.

Though deep down inside, so deep I can hardly admit it to myself, there's the fact that her ability to swoop in and take control is a massive turn on. This is new. A facet of myself I didn't know existed until today. Sure, a capable, intelligent woman has always interested me—I've never gone for the bubbleheads who can't hold a conversation beyond the latest gossip about celebrities they'll never meet. Granted, they might make for a fun night in bed, but that's where it ends.

This woman, on the other hand? Not only is she smart as hell, but I can't shake the suspicion that she would be a wildcat in the sack. All her intensity, all her passion, it would just have to translate into a wild time. Nothing could convince me otherwise.

Together, we'd be explosive. And now, lucky me, I have an excuse to spend time with her.

“You look pleased with yourself.”

Her wry observation cuts its way through my inner thoughts, and I look her way to find her smirking. “Congratulating yourself?” she asks while her thumbs continue to move across her screen.

“How do you do that?”

"Do what? It's not difficult to read the expression you're wearing."

"That's not what I meant." *Note to self: pay more attention to your face.* "I meant you're typing. How do you do it without looking at the screen?"

The question must take her by surprise, since a soft laugh bubbles out of her before she looks down at her screen. "I don't know. Practice?"

"It's fascinating."

"I'm glad you find me interesting." She clears her throat, her gaze lowered to her phone again. "I need to send a message to my partner to let her know we are going ahead with this."

"Did you tell her all about what a monster I am?"

"And what if I did?" She pierces me with an unforgiving glare. "Considering you're in the position you're in, maybe you shouldn't make jokes about things like that."

"You're right. My apologies." Even if it does raise my hackles, she's quick to chastise me. I hope she doesn't get it in her head that I'm going to roll over and let her walk all over me in those stilettos.

There's a limit to my patience, and while she might have my balls in a vice, there are certain lines I can't let her cross.

I'm glad she's on her phone, really. It gives me a chance to study her without her staring back at me. Even knowing who she used to be, I can't make that memory align with what I see in front of me now. This polished, professional smokeshow is as far away from Wallowing Willow as anyone could be.

Just the memory of that nickname makes me shudder—I'm disappointed in myself, and not only because I would very much like to bend her over this desk and fuck her senseless. This goes deeper than ruining my chances of getting laid.

I have to wonder if some of what I see in front of me isn't because of the way I humiliated her. Did she have something to prove because of my bullying? Then again, look how far she's come. I could just as easily congratulate myself for being the reason for it.

If I were a complete asshole, that is.

"Alright. That's out of the way." She looks up quickly, and I have to pretend I wasn't staring. "Now. Next steps."

"Why don't we head downstairs for a late lunch?" I suggest fixing my tie. "We could discuss a schedule down there, and our kitchen is damn near legendary."

Her face goes stony. "Absolutely not."

"Is that how this is going to go? You can work with me, but you can't be seen with me?"

She rolls her eyes, sighing like she's dealing with a petulant child. "If we're going to work together, you're going to need to put your ego aside for a minute. I'm sure that's foreign, but give it a try."

"Just because I'm at your mercy doesn't mean I'm going to put up with snark morning, noon, and night."

Her lips twitch but she overlooks it. "The point is, the last thing you want to do right now is be seen enjoying yourself in public. I'm not saying you have to walk around whipping yourself for everyone to see, but you don't need more negative opinions being thrown your way. Does that make sense?"

"Yes. I see your point." And now I wish I hadn't jumped to conclusions. There's an unspoken battle raging between us, both of us fighting for control. She's won this battle, rolling her eyes at me, knocking me down a peg.

That doesn't mean she's going to win the war.

"If you're that hungry, we can eat here in your office. But keep that in mind going forward, until all of this has passed. You might want to pump the brakes on your social life."

"Understood." Really, I wasn't inviting her to lunch strictly to discuss business. I want to talk about her. Who she is, where she comes from, what makes her tick. Whether she's getting off on being in control and whether that has anything to do with feeling out of control when she was a kid.

Now, she's the one with all the power, the one telling people what to do while they have no choice but to obey. I can see how that would be a turn-on for someone who was treated the way I treated her.

At least I know she's professional, always thinking about the task at hand. We haven't even signed a contract yet, but she's already on the job.

As if she reads my mind, she glances up from her phone again. "I guess we should discuss contracts at this point."

"Have you brought one with you?"

"I'll send it your way now." Again, she taps away on her phone, her red nails shining in the light. "It's sent."

"I'll print it." While standing, I add, "Why don't you check out the website for the club. The menu’s there. Whatever you'd like, I can have it sent up.”

“Thanks. I guess I could use a little something.” Of course, because she wasn't planning on staying. No doubt she'd be well on her way back to Manhattan by now if this had gone the way she’d planned.

“It's probably not as exciting as what I'm sure you could get delivered in your neighborhood.”

“It'll be just fine.” She's hardly paying attention to a word I've said, still too involved with her phone. I'm doing my best to learn a little bit about her and where she lives, how she is, and I'm not even sure why it seems so important that I learn all there is to know. Clearly, she is not interested in providing answers. Again, I have to remind myself we aren't here to socialize, no matter how intriguing I find her.

It isn't until I head to Theresa's office that I remember she's here. “I'll take that,” I announce, pulling the contract from her printer. “I might need you to type up a few changes depending on what we negotiate, but I’ll make sure it doesn’t take too long. You’re already doing me a favor by being here on a Saturday.”

"Well? How did it go? I didn't hear any screaming, so I assume that's a good thing?"

"It came very close to screams," I admit in a whisper. "But it's a success."

"Oh, thank goodness," she whispers, one hand to her chest. "I'll be offering prayers of thanks during services tomorrow."

"Throw an extra one in there for me, will you?" With that, I hustle down the hall to where Willow now peruses our menu. There is something inherently graceful about her—it's the way she holds her head, her posture, and if I didn't know better I would think she was a dancer in her younger days. Wallowing Willow was not a dancer.

Though for all I know, she could have been. She seemed clumsy and awkward when we were young, but I'm sure my criticism didn't help things. I only made her feel that way, I suppose. I wonder if it's possible to make up for something like that, and whether she would let me try. She seems to have a lot of pride, that much is for sure, so I doubt she would open up easily.

"I'll have a cobb salad," she decides before accepting her copy of the contract while I sit down with the other copy. I call down the order, along with a chicken sandwich for myself, before turning my full attention to the contract.

"I would like to get this done with as soon as possible," I murmur while scanning the contents. "My secretary was kind enough to come in today, and I'd like to let her go home soon."

"Is that your way of trying to rush me through This? Using your secretary to hurry me up?"

"No matter what you might think, not everything I do has an ulterior motive."

"We'll see about that." There's a smile playing at the corners of her mouth but she keeps her head lowered, staring down at a contract that, I'm sure, she's already familiar with.

"Fifty percent deposit in advance?" I whistle softly.

"What, too much? And here I was, thinking the Cargills had all the money in the world."

"You realize we're not going to get very far if you keep making personal comments. Ball-bustingI can handle, but you seem to be going out of your way."

"Fair enough, but those are my terms. And I don't negotiate when it comes to that."

“I wasn't complaining,” I feel the need to remind her. She loves having me on the defensive, so I can’t make it too easy for her. It's like every moment we spend together, I find myself fighting to get my footing. Otherwise there's nothing for me to do but slide helplessly along shifting sand while she stands above me, watching me struggle.

She's got a chip on her shoulder. I have to remember that, and I have to accept it. With time, that will ease… I hope.

Especially since she is so damn tempting. Buttoned up, ultra professional, but seething inside. There's part of me, not even very far beneath the surface, determined to make her explode.

“And what's this clause?” I ask, pointing to the section in question and willing myself not to stare at the narrow strip of chest exposed by the button she left open on her blouse. “You can decide at any time to end this agreement?”

“That's right, and I keep the deposit.”

“And your clients generally go for this?”

“Let's get something straight.” She lowers the paper to her lap, squaring her shoulders like she's ready for battle. How much has this girl had to fight that she's always so ready for the next one? “I am going to tell you what to do based upon my expertise, and you are going to do exactly as I say. I'm entering into this agreement in good faith. However, if at any point you decide you know better than I do, it's a waste of time for both of us to continue working together. And believe me," she adds with a smirk, "that clause wouldn't be in there if I hadn't already been burned."

"Really?"

She lifts a shoulder, trying to play it off even while her mouth is set in a scowl. "In the early days, I figured it was enough to trust my clients to follow my advice. Most of them did, but there were a few who thought they knew better. And when they didn't get results, who do you think they blamed?"

She points a thumb at herself, grimacing. "So then there came the arguments about whether they should pay the rest of my fee, because clearly I didn't know what I was talking about if they were still having trouble."

"So you decided to hell with it," I conclude.

"Something like that. If you aren't going to work with me, then I am not going to work with you. End of story."

"I admire that."

She arches an eyebrow, looking me up and down. “Really?”

“Yes, really. It takes guts to stand up for yourself. And you're right—some people will never learn. You can't twist yourself into a pretzel trying to make them happy when they won't meet you halfway.”

“That's right.” There's a wicked gleam in her eyes. “Don't think I won't remind you of that the first time you decide you don't like my advice.”

“I would expect nothing less.” Otherwise, I see nothing else to argue. Once we've agreed on the terms, I send the contract to Theresa with a few instructions, along with the routing numbers for the deposit. The timing couldn't be better, as moments later there's a knock at the door to signal our lunch has arrived.

“I don't want you to think I haven't given this any thought on my own.” Just why I feel the need to prove myself is a mystery, but one that I can't help giving in to before taking a bite of my sandwich.

“What do you mean?” she asks, spearing lettuce and hard-boiled egg on her fork.

“I did some research on my own, before you got here.”

"Oh, you did?"

"Why do you sound like you're about to laugh?"

"Do I?" It's clear she's having fun with this, barely bothering to hide a grin while she eats.

"I didn't want to leave it all up to you, and I wanted to approach this in good faith."

"Bravo." She lifts an eyebrow, clearly waiting for more.

"From what I read, it's advised to make an apology, something official. Then, to improve my image, I could donate to a local charity organization. Something committed to the local area—I want to remind everyone how committed I am to Somerset Harbor, not only to the club."

She doesn't say a word, taking another forkful of food and chewing slowly.

"Maybe I should post something to my Instagram?" I suggest.

"No," she barks, her head swinging from side to side.

"Why not?"

She sets down her fork with a sigh. "You don't want people to be curious about why you're apologizing and go to look for the video. Right?"

Now that she puts it that way, I could kick myself for bringing it up. "Okay. Point taken."

"Now, from what you've said, this hasn't become as much of a disaster as it could be, because the problem is still somewhat limited. In fact, when I went searching for the video online after you reached out, I didn't see many mentions of your name. Yes, it's a mess, but it's not like you are being vilified across the entire internet. It's only here, in Somerset Harbor, where people really care. So we need to keep it local, and make small, deliberate steps rather than a blanket apology on a social media platform where most of your followers are strangers who might not even know about this."

"Of course. See? This is why you're the expert."

"You don't need to tell me that." She inclines her head toward a notepad on the desk. "Write down everywhere the video exists—every platform, that is—and I'll have my people start taking it down."

"Just like that?"

"Just like that."

"But how?"

"Like you said, that's why I'm the expert."

Touché.

"I have my ways," she continues, relenting a little. "At least, they do, and I just happen to hire the right people. Don't worry about it. Within hours, the video will be scrubbed from the internet." As she speaks, she holds her fork in one hand, her phone in the other, and her thumb moves across the screen while she stabs a piece of chicken. The woman is the ultimate multitasker.

"Thank you."

She gives me the briefest glance, almost like she's annoyed to be interrupted. "This is my job, remember."

"And if you check, you'll find a pending deposit to your account."

Now that gets her attention. "Thank you. I appreciate promptness."

I wish she wouldn't be so buttoned up and businesslike. It's not going to be easy, breaking down her walls. I'm not even sure why it matters so much—if anything, it would be smart to keep this on a purely professional level. This is too important to screw up by making it personal.

Though to be fair, it's been personal from the beginning, but that's my fault. If she has a chip on her shoulder, I put it there years before I knew I would ever need her. I wish I could go back and slap that version of myself straight upside the head. The arrogant little prick.

"So what do I do?" I ask, sitting back and groaning in frustration.

"You?" She looks up from her phone, her lips drawn into a thin, disapproving line. "Nothing. You don't do a damned thing unless I tell you to do it." I almost can't believe the intensity in her gaze as she pins me to my chair without laying a hand on me. "Understood?"

The only thing I understand at this moment is how desperate I am to break down the walls between us. Since I can't exactly say that out loud, I settle for nodding while energy crackles between us. "Understood."

"Remember, you hired me for a job. Let me do my work so you can focus on yours."

"Fair enough." But what she doesn't understand, what she couldn't possibly comprehend, is the importance of another job that's now made itself abundantly clear.

Finding a way to make up for all the pain I caused her, since that's the only way to make our arrangement more than strictly professional.

14

WILLOW

"Damn it. I should have been out of here ten minutes ago."

"You're running around here like a chicken with your head cut off," Sarah observes from the doorway to my office.

"And you aren't doing much to make me feel better."

She pauses, then begins slowly clapping like we're at a golf tournament. "Yay. You're doing great."

"You're lucky I like you." Finally, I find my phone under a pile of newspapers and magazines. I like to go through them to keep an eye out on current events, gossip, that sort of thing. I can always tell when a good PR specialist is on the job. It's sort of a superpower of mine. Years spent spinning stories in my client's favor have left me with a sharp eye.

"I didn't know he'd want so many hours, but then I guess he figures he's bought it."

She's not kidding about Sawyer wanting my time. This has been the longest week of my life, and instead of being able to go home and unwind on a Friday night, I have to drive up to Somerset Harbor for a meeting with the handful of city council members who've reached out to Sawyer over the past several days. It took a little bit of sweet talking, but I managed to reach out to each of them individually and convince them to come to dinner at the club.

The idea of once again making the drive up and back leaves me feeling more tired than I already did. "I should rent a place up there. It would save on mileage."

"Or you could stay with Sawyer."

The hint of humor she can't hide leaves me glaring at her. "Don't even joke about that."

"Sure, of course." Still, her lips twitch like she's trying to hold back a laugh.

"It's not funny. I hate him, you know this." I throw my phone into my bag with a grunt. "All week, it's been like managing a toddler. He always wants to go off on a whim without thinking things over."

"He thinks he's being proactive."

"He's being a pain in the ass," I grumble. "I swear, if I get through this without killing him, it'll be a miracle."

"Or kissing him."

"One more wisecrack, and I swear..."

"Okay, fine. But let's not pretend you aren't wearing your hottest outfit for this meeting."

I look down at my black sheath dress, biting my lip. I can't pretend I didn't deliberately choose the dress that leaves me feeling powerful and confident, but sexy? "You think it's my hottest outfit?"

"You look fantastic, and you know it. That's the dress you wear when you want to impress people." She folds her arms, arching an eyebrow. "Add to that the pearl necklace and the Cartier watch, and it looks to me like you're pulling out all the stops."

Her mention of my watch makes me check it, and I cringe harder than before. "I really need to go—or else he'll end up doing something stupid before I get there." I practically run for the door, and not only because I'm late. It's not that I'm trying to avoid Sarah's insightful jokes. It's just that I don't feel like listening to them.

She's got a talent for reading me like a book. She sees the difference in me this week. Sawyer is at the front of my mind all the time, every day, thanks to his talent for annoying me and almost screwing up everything I'm trying to put in place.

"Why do I have to hide in my office all the time?" That was my favorite question this week. The big baby. Acting like I'm locking him up.

"What do you mean, I have to host the city council at the club?" There I was, thinking he possessed a modicum of intelligence. If he did, he wouldn't have to ask me that.

"You mean I can't post anything to my Instagram?" That was when I was pretty convinced he's deliberately trolling, trying to get under my skin. I had to remind him of our conversation over the weekend when I told him in no uncertain terms to stay off social media. Not only in relation to the video, but in general. It's better for him to lay low until this blows over. That means no pictures of him on his yacht, or sitting in his office, or kissing up to the guests.

"Absolutely ridiculous," I grumble to myself once I'm in my car, peeling out of the garage.

I’d ask myself how he managed to get as far as he has while running on two good brain cells, but I know the answer. He happens to be a Cargill.

Because I'm running a little late, I call his secretary to let her know. It's safer that way. “Theresa, it's Willow Anderson.”

“As if I didn't know your voice by now,” she points out with a gentle laugh. I like her. After years of dealing with protective, gatekeeping assistants, she's a breath of fresh air. “What can I do for you?”

“I wanted to let Sawyer know I'm running a little late. Not terribly, and I'll be there on time for the dinner. Just in case he was wondering, though.”

“I'll let him know. Be careful out there. Don't worry about getting here on time. Just get here in one piece.”

“Yes, ma'am.” I'm grinning as I end the call. At least there's one reasonable person working at the club. Sawyer has already explained that Theresa used to work for his father, and I can't help but wonder if the old man left her in place to keep an eye on his son. I wouldn't be a bit surprised. I've known enough wealthy men to understand how they think. He might have put his son in the driver's seat, but Theresa is there as a reminder not to drive too fast.

It's not another two minutes before my phone rings, and I'm not surprised to find who's calling. "What do you mean, you're running late?" Sawyer's voice fills the car, setting my teeth on edge even while the rest of my body responds in the worst possible way.

In spite of my tight nipples and the heat rising in my core, I manage somehow to keep my voice level. "Exactly what part of that statement is giving you a hard time?"

"You're the one who wanted to have this dinner in the first place."

"Correct."

"And you can't even bother to be on time?"

"There is plenty of time," I grit out, my hands tightening around the wheel. "I won't be there early, is all."

"Maybe we should postpone."

"Are you out of your mind? What part of this is so hard for you to understand? I decided to pay you the courtesy of a phone call to let you know I'm running later than expected. This is not a situation where we postpone the meeting. Do not, I repeat, do not make any rash decisions."

"I still think it would have been better to have one-on-one meetings."

"Remind me who's being paid to do this job? Because all week long, it seems like you've been getting mixed up. I know what I'm doing."

"Can you explain to me why it's so important to get everybody together so they can stare me down?"

This again. I have to remind myself he's not deliberately being ignorant, but rather voicing his stress and fear. No, he would never openly admit to being afraid, but it's pretty obvious from where I'm sitting.

"If anybody is on the fence about whether or not to accept your apology, they will be swayed by positive reactions from others. It's human psychology. If this person and that person think things are okay, maybe they are."

"You do realize the same can work just as well in reverse, right? What if this person and that person told me to go fuck myself?"

"The way I did, more than once? Maybe you can wear them down the way you wore me down."

"Cute."

"I'm not trying to be cute. I'm trying to prove a point. You can be very persuasive when you put your mind to it—even charming."

Wrong choice of words, you idiot. "You think I'm charming?"

"I think you have the potential to be charming under the correct circumstances."

"You make me feel like I'm reading from a science textbook."

"Are we finished? Because I would like to focus on the road. It is rush hour, you realize. If I wrap my car around a pole, you'll have to get through the mess you created all on your own. We don't want that, do we?"

He definitely grumbles something that sounds close to profanity. "Should I get things rolling without you if you're held up?"

"Good God, no. Anything but that."

"Thanks. I'm glad you have all this faith in me."

"It's not a matter of faith." It's totally a matter of faith. "I want to be there to steer the conversation."

"But you're not going to run things."

It almost hurts to roll my eyes so hard. "No. I will not try to run things. You're still in charge, big shot."

"You're right. I am a big shot. So long as you don't forget that." And then he ends the call because he is a dick who always has to have the last word. All I can do is growl helplessly and wish I had never accepted this job in the first place. There's no amount of money worth the wringer he's putting me through.

I don't know where he got the idea that I want to banter with him. Didn't I make it clear enough that I can't stand the sight of his face? His ridiculously symmetrical, chiseled face? Maybe I'm not being hard enough on him.

And I guess I could be faulted for taking the bait he dangles in front of me. I don't know what it is about him that makes me want to knock him down a peg or two, but it always ends with me wishing I hadn't engaged in the first place. Somehow, he winds up on top.

He's a spoiled, entitled little slug with the inexplicable power to turn me on with the lift of a single eyebrow. Hell, I'm still ridiculously aroused and we were only on the phone. And I was annoyed with him. How does he do it?

That doesn't matter. I need to get my head in the game, and fast, since I have no choice but to be professional in front of a bunch of old men who hold my client's future in their hands. This has nothing to do with my personal feelings toward Sawyer or our past.

I have a job to do, and nobody does it better than me.

So long as I can convince my client to stop shooting himself in the foot, I'm golden.

15

SAWYER

"Where is she?" I can't help but check the window again, hoping to find her headlights cutting through the darkness that's begun to fall. Once again, I'm disappointed. It seems that's the nature of things anymore.

"There's still plenty of time before the meeting."

The only thing keeping me from lashing out at my brother is the reminder of what this means to him. Brooks is as much a part of this business as I am, and I'm well aware of the slight downtick in events. Normally at this time of year, he's hurrying around like a chicken without his head, trying to squeeze yet another prospective guest meeting into his already overbooked schedule.

I continue staring out the window behind my desk to conceal the sour expression I'm wearing. "Yes, I know. But I was hoping I could get a little time with her before that, to go over some things."

"You seem to have a firm grip on the talking points Willow sent over." Naturally, I sent them his way for a second opinion. Usually, I'd trust my instincts, but this is not a normal situation. Not even close.

I turn to him, where he stands in front of my desk in his usual dark suit. If there's one thing Dad taught us, it was how to uphold an image. He exudes calm confidence—and he can, because this isn't all riding on him. He's not the one lying in bed at night, imagining his employees working at the new Macmillan resort once we close our doors for good.

The very idea makes my temples throb. Because I need to heap more self-loathing onto an already bitterly fraught situation.

"I'm sure you're right." Because, in the end, what's the good of arguing? I only come off looking like a child. And he is right. I made it a point to study what Willow sent over in prep for the meeting, regardless of how it grates on my nerves that I have to smile like a good boy and keep my mouth shut except when I'm repeating what I've been told to say.

The grin my brother wears, reflected in the window, isn't helping things. He has to know how this is twisting my balls. I appreciate him believing I'll get through it, but his obvious glee at not being the guy in the hot seat makes me grind my molars.

"If you don't mind, I'm going to head out. Unless… you want me to stick around?"

It's that added question that softens me and eases the tightness in my chest enough that I'm able to breathe. Brooks is always ready with a quip or a smartass remark, but that's surface bullshit.

"Why would I need you?" I smirk at him over my shoulder for lack of courage. I want to thank him. I want to ask his advice. All I can do is watch him roll his eyes before offering a knowing smirk of his own.

"Don't say I never offered." With that, he whistles his way out of my office, his footsteps light.

"Where are you headed tonight?" I call out, wishing I could be so carefree.

"I thought I'd grab dinner at Quinn's place and bully him into going out for drinks." His best friend runs a popular seafood restaurant in town, and their nights out usually involve one of them acting as wingman while the other picks up his latest conquest.

"No dinner and drinks here?"

He laughs while rounding the door jamb. "I don't shit where I eat, brother." In other words, tonight will involve women. I suppose I should be grateful he's not picking up a daughter of one of our members.

That leaves me alone, fighting to maintain my self-control.

This is nothing. I have to be charming. I know how to turn it on and off—it's a huge part of my job. Making sure our guests feel at home, welcome, valued. If Dad taught me anything, it was how to smile my way through even the most uncomfortable situations.

Has there ever been a more uncomfortable situation than the one I'm facing now? The idea of eating crow in front of these judgmental pains in the ass leaves me with a pain in my chest worse than any heartburn. If Willow were here, she'd call it the pain of a wounded ego.

But she's not here, is she? Yet I can't help but hear her voice in my head. There's a good chance I need professional help.

No, the solution to the silencing voice I hear whether I want to or not is much simpler.

The fact I'll admit to nobody but myself is this, I'm not anxious for her to get here only for the sake of the meeting. Sure, I need her for it—more than I like, much more—but I would wait for her with bated breath no matter why she was on her way.

And the solution can only be to finally take her, the way I've fantasized about doing all week. Taking her until she weeps with pleasure and sobs my name. Breaking down that wall she puts up around herself.

Only Willow could leave me with a semi stirring in my pants at a moment like this.

Focus. I don't need a surprise boner getting in the way of my concentration tonight. There's way too much riding on this.

Riding. Terrific. I have to squeeze my eyes closed and clench my fists and will away the mental image of Willow on top of me. I've never seen what's beneath those buttoned-up suits she wears, but I can imagine. I have done much more than my fair share of imagining. Staring, too, though this week we've worked via phone and text for the most part. I've had to rely on memories, though there are plenty of those. I did my fair share of staring when she was here.

Tonight will be my first time seeing her face-to-face since our nearly disastrous meeting in this office. My heart races and my palms are sweaty and if I didn't know better, I would think I'm waiting to pick up my date for the big dance.

No. I wasn't even this bad back then.

And I wish I hadn't thought of that, because now I have the memory of our senior dance to reflect on. One more thing to berate myself over.

If only I hadn't been so damn stupid and childish. Every time I look back on that night, which I've done more times than I can count in the past several days, I cringe a little harder than before. Why did I do that? The girl never hurt me. She meant nothing to me and pretty much minded her own business as far as I can recall. I saw someone small, weak, and vulnerable, and I pounced.

What does that say about me? It's enough to make me wonder if she knows me better than I know myself. She's seen my worst parts, the aspects of my personality which I'd rather bury. Unlike me, she faces them head-on rather than pretend they don't exist.

My breath catches at the sight of headlights sweeping over the driveway, but the car doesn't belong to her. There's a pit in my stomach that gets a little larger with every passing moment, until the Porsche is illuminated by tasteful lights positioned at even intervals around the circular courtyard in front of the main entrance. I know that car, having seen it zipping around town for years. It's Rob Myers' baby, and many times I've passed his house to find him waxing it in the driveway. The head of the city council and a real hard ass, he's the one whose approval I need most of all.

Another pair of headlights soon catches my eye, and I watch once again. Let it be her. Please, let it be her. She's arrogant, chilly, still holding me at arm's length, but I need her. It's that simple. I need her to talk me off the ledge before this meeting starts. The idea is to allow everyone to mingle at the bar before I go down to lead them to the table reserved for us by the back windows. If I wanted to, I'm sure I could keep them waiting—it would give them more time to talk amongst themselves, though, and I'm not sure I want to do that, either. No sense in giving them the chance to make up their minds on what a shithead I am.

The sight of her stepping out of the car upon parking in front of the club is magic. Instantly, the tension that's been knotting my muscles all day dissolves. I sink into my chair, a little weak kneed, laughing softly in relief. Thank God. I don't have to go through this alone.

Still, I need to keep it together. I can't have her finding me shaking like a leaf all because she decided to get here at a reasonable time. Sitting up straight, I adjust my tie, then smooth my hair back with both hands. She kept me waiting. I can't have her thinking that's acceptable.

No sooner had she stepped through the doorway than I snort, looking her up and down. "Thanks for deciding to grace me with your presence."

She stops short, and the way her head snaps back pairs well with her narrowed eyes.

"I'll have you know I came real close to earning myself a speeding ticket out there. Try not to be such a baby." She sets her bag down on the leather sofa and rolls her head from side to side like she's working out stiffness. "If I could have gotten here any faster, I would have."

"Maybe you should have left earlier."

"Maybe the entire world doesn't revolve around you, Sawyer. Try to keep that in mind, okay? We want you to act at least semi-human in front of these people, or you're only going to make things worse."

She checks the time—I can't help but admire her watch along with the rest of her. "Besides, I looked around down there and there are still a few missing members. Are you going to give them shit, too?"

"Alright," I grumble. Why is it I can never get the upper hand with her? If I didn't know better, I would think she plans out her reactions in advance. If that were true, it would mean I'm too predictable. Am I?

This is not the time for me to start second guessing my every thought.

"You look nice," I offer.

Her mouth sets in a smirk while she scrolls through something on her phone. "Thank you for your approval."

"Is it so wrong to offer a compliment?"

Her smirk only deepens when she lifts her head, quirking an eyebrow. "Maybe I'm just not used to hearing them from you."

This again. There's a very large part of me that wants to tell her to get over it, but I can't afford to push her away. There's letting my mouth get away from me, and there's shooting myself in the foot. "Well, you do," I offer again, this time in a softer voice.

"Thanks." She touches a hand to the pearls around her neck, and unless I'm mistaken there's a flush on her cheeks by the time she returns her attention to her phone. "According to what I saw downstairs, comparing them to the photos I found online, we are missing Ed Saunders and Craig Davis. The others are down there."

"You looked them up online?"

"I believe in being prepared." Finally she lowers her phone, favoring me with a full stare. "Did you think I was kidding when I said I knew what I'm doing? I have to research my opponents."

"And you consider them opponents?"

"Right now, yes. They stand in the way of you getting what you want, and that goes far beyond granting approval to expand your dining room. You want their approval, their acceptance, and you want this to blow over. That means knowing who we're dealing with and how to get through to them short of getting on our knees and begging."

I'd love to get her on her knees.

I need a cold shower.

Not for the first time, I wonder if there'd be any chance of spending time together one-on-one after this is all over. Right now, I doubt it—she's about as icy as the harbor in the heart of January.

But damn, that dress and the body it covers has my mind moving in directions it absolutely should not explore at a time like this. I won't be able to get her out of my head until I'm able to indulge in those curves, and that's the problem in a nutshell. If I could have her, I could forget her. The novelty would be gone, and with it my interest. That's the way it usually is.

And here she is, practically wearing a sign that says Do Not Touch hanging from those pearls of hers.

"Are you ready for this?" She takes a step back, tipping her head to the side. "You look good, too. I noticed you got a haircut."

"You do have an eye for detail, don't you?"

"It's my job." She takes a deep breath, gesturing for me to do the same. I follow her lead, feeling like a fool. "Now. What do you need to remember tonight?"

"Do we have to do this?"

"No. I'm in the habit of asking questions I don't expect answers to. Tell me. What do you need to remember tonight?"

"You're enjoying this, aren't you?"

"I'm doing my job." Yes, and she is entirely full of shit because she is most definitely enjoying this. She can't even be bothered to hide a grin.

With a heavy sigh, I repeat what she's drilled into my head the past week. "I can't have everything the way I want it exactly when I want it."

"And why is that?"

My jaw's beginning to ache from all the teeth grinding. "Because I don't run the world."

"And?"

"And I need to be nice to people if I want them to give me what I want."

"Close enough."

"What? Isn't that what you have drilled into my hand?"

"Actually, what I told you was, you might be a big fish in a small pond, but in the grand scheme of things you are not that important."

"Do you sweet talk all of your clients this way, or do you reserve that kindness for me?"

"I'm trying to give you a sense of proportion. I realize your situation feels like the end of the world, like everywhere you go, people are looking at you. But that just isn't true. And if you can see it that way, it can be easier to take a breath and look at this situation from the outside. That's where you can think strategically, from the outside, not when you are neck deep in drama."

"Alright, fair enough."

My desk phone rings, and the double chime tells me it's a call from somewhere in the building. "Mr. Cargill, all of your guests are down here."

"Thank you." Just like that, there's ice in my stomach, threatening to freeze me in place.

"Are you ready for this?" Willow asks, and for once there is no sarcastic note to her voice, no smirk.

"You tell me. Do you think I'm ready?"

"The truth?"

"Would you give me anything less?"

"I think you are capable of great things so long as you remember to stay out of your own way."

It's funny. The hardest fought compliments are the ones that mean the most. A man like me is easily surrounded by yes men, by inconsequential strangers hoping to score access to wealth and prestige. In other words, I hear compliments a lot.

Yet for the first time in as long as I can remember, I feel bolstered by her observation.

“Okay.” Squaring my shoulders, I head for the elevator. “Let's do this.”

16

WILLOW

I have to wonder if the man isn't a real-life Jekyll and Hyde.

When all I've seen, both in the past and present, is the self-centered, egotistical, all important silver spoon rich kid, the sight of a very charming, charismatic Sawyer just about knocks me off my feet. Or out of my chair, rather, while I sit at his right hand and marvel at how easily he turns the charm on and off as he sees fit. If I didn't know better, I'd think he has serious personality issues.

Who am I kidding? He definitely has issues.

But if I didn't know him as well as I do, I might actually be taken with him.

"Bottom line," grunts Rob Myers. He leans back in his chair to my left, clinking the ice in his glass. "There're lots of people in town who aren't sold on the idea of expanding this place. Now, your feelings about the townsfolk aside, what do you propose to do about that?"

Sawyer clears his throat, his dark eyes meeting mine for a split second. "With the help of Miss Anderson, we plan to launch a campaign in the town to win them over on the benefits of an expansion. This is more than a matter of a healthy bottom line. Not only would it make it easier for our members to enjoy dining here with their friends and loved ones, but it would give us greater options and flexibility for events. Weddings, showers, parties. We want to play a bigger part in the community. We want as many happy memories tied to the yacht club as possible."

He even manages to sound sincere.

Maybe I'm being too hard on him. The fact is, I hear the sincerity throbbing in his voice. I believe he believes it, that he wants his family's legacy to involve more than money and exclusivity. He wants to play a part in something bigger.

Maybe I need to believe that, or else why am I here?

Rob snorts. "Happy memories with a bunch of... what did you call us again?"

I can almost hear Sawyer's teeth grinding. Keep it together. I warned you about this. Obviously, there was going to be at least one outlier who wasn't willing or able to smile politely and enjoy a free meal. A delicious meal, too, with salmon so buttery it practically melts in my mouth. He wasn't kidding about the level of skill in the kitchen.

I have to give it to him. He knows how to hide his irritation when it counts. Rather than lash out, he simply lowers his cutlery to his plate, then dabs the corners of his mouth with a napkin. Taking time to get his thoughts together. These are all good signs. Is this how Doctor Frankenstein felt when he watched his monster?

"I'm glad you brought that up," he murmurs with something close to a genuine smile. "Let's address the elephant in the room, shall we? The fact that when I've had too much to drink, I tend to make an ass out of myself."

At least two of the men around the table choke softly before clearing their throats, while the rest merely chuckle. "And I say whichever one of us has never been guilty of that can throw the first stone," he continues. "It was not my finest moment, and I apologize. I was frustrated. As you know, taking this position means living up to pretty high standards. I'm living under a large, large shadow. I'm eager to prove myself—and at the moment, after finding out it would take more time and effort than I had imagined to expand, I was frustrated and angry. From where I stood, my plans to prove to the board that I was the correct choice for CEO to replace my father were being thwarted. This means much more to me than a mere expansion, gentlemen. I responded accordingly."

I think that's as honest as I've heard him speak about himself all week.

And damn it, when he puts it that way, I almost feel sorry for him. Okay, so he's a poor little rich boy. I can't have much sympathy for somebody who's had their entire life handed to them on a silver platter.

But he's also a human being. And he wants to prove himself.

Who is this man, really?

One thing is for sure, I don't need to be as active a participant in this meeting as I first imagined. Sure, there have been a few sour looks, but for the most part he's got everything well in hand. It occurs to me that in situations like this, he's got the advantage. That doesn't happen often.

He knows these men because he's one of them. He understands what they respond to because he's grown up around them. The men range in age, but for the most part could be his father's contemporaries. That might also explain why they were the ones who were so deeply offended by the video that they felt it necessary to call and complain, which inspired this dinner meeting in the first place. They don't want some young, cocky little nothing criticizing them.

He can handle them because he can handle his father. He's probably made a career of it, he and his brothers. Now I find myself wanting to meet them, to see if they share his innate ability to placate the egos of older, somewhat cranky men.

I sort of wonder if they're all as good looking as him, too.

Not what I need to be thinking about right now. Not even close.

"I understand that's why you hired this lovely young woman." Rob turns to me, and I'm sure he thinks his smile is charming. Coming from a seventy-three-year-old man with grandchildren close to my age, it's damn creepy. "If I knew it would mean working with someone like you, I might run my mouth at the wrong time, too."

Is it possible to hear a person's hackles rise? If so, that's what I'm hearing from Sawyer. He's practically growling while I offer a calm, polite smile. "I can't guarantee my schedule will be open," I murmur.

"I'm sure we could work something out."

"I hate to break it to you," Sawyer interjects, "but I'm keeping her very busy. I'm incorrigible and she'll be the first one to tell you so."

"Incorrigible?" I tap my chin like I'm thinking. "I can think of a few words I would use before I would land on that one." Soft laughter rises up over the table. Even Sawyer joins in, and he almost sounds genuine.

Sawyer Cargill, laughing at himself? I might need to take the weekend off to recover from the shock.

I might also need the time to get my hormones in check, because I can't stop staring at his mouth. The way it ticks upward at the corner when he hears something he disagrees with but knows better than to verbalize. The way it twists into a scowl when he hears something he doesn't like—I get that one a lot, obviously. Its generous contours, not to mention the dimple that appears on the rare occasions when he smiles.

What would it be like...

No. Stop. Absolutely not.

But he did go out of his way to compliment my appearance tonight. And I can't pretend I didn't see the look in his eyes when he said it. I might have spent a lot of time being out of shape and generally unattractive thanks to having no clue how to manage my hair and no money to get Lasik, but I got my act together in college and men noticed the way men tend to do.

In other words, I've seen that look before. I know what it means.

And maybe it's because I'm a weak idiot, or maybe because I haven't gone on anything resembling a proper date in longer than I care to remember, but I found myself feeling giddy and fluttery inside. It took everything I had not to show it, and I think I did alright, but who knows?

"Really," he continues, smiling my way, "I don't know what I would have done if it weren't for Willow. She's kept me centered through all of this craziness—craziness of my own making," he concludes with a self-deprecating grin which turns into a full-fledged, warm smile once he directs his gaze my way.

Is that my heart skipping a beat? The worst part is, I can't deflect the way I normally would with a snarky comment or a roll of my eyes since we're not alone. There's nothing to do but absorb that warmth and fight like hell to make sure it doesn't translate to heat in my core.

Whoops. Too late. As usual, my body's determined to sabotage me. Pressing my thighs together does nothing to ease the throbbing that's now beginning to distract me.

I wonder if he'll ask me back up to his office to celebrate a successful meeting, which this seems to be. I wonder if I should accept. Should I place that sort of temptation in my path? Because once we're alone, celebrating a win, it would be all too easy to let my guard down and let him do whatever he wants.

It's a fantasy, pure and simple. I don't even know if he would take that step. But in my imagination? Oh, yes. He takes that step. He takes a lot of steps, in fact.

He pushes me onto the leather couch and kisses his way up the insides of my thighs until he finally makes contact with my aching, throbbing bundle of nerves.

He parts my lips and drags his tongue through my wetness, while I moan his name and run my fingers through his thick, soft hair.

He strips every piece of clothing off me and explores my body with his hands, his lips, his tongue. All of that before he finally claims me with his—

It's the sharp clearing of his throat that snaps me back to reality. My cheeks are flushed, my pulse racing, and one furtive glance toward the man who lives at the center of my fantasies doesn't exactly help things.

Because there is something lurking in those dark depths that gives me a sneaking suspicion he knew exactly what I was thinking about.

That's not possible. I have gone out of my way—I mean to the point where I'm practically twisting myself into a pretzel—to make sure he's clueless when it comes to this insane yearning I have for him. A yearning so intense I almost hate myself for it because I'm better than this. Aren't I? What's wrong with me that I'm practically creaming my panties over someone who destroyed my self-esteem and made me a laughingstock?

When he won't stop with that knowing look he insists on giving me, all I can do is narrow my eyes at him.

And the arrogant son of a bitch has the nerve to smile.

Once again, like everything else in his life, I'm making it way too easy for him. It's enough to make me wonder if he hasn't been deliberately getting under my skin all week. He obviously seems to enjoy knocking me off my game, watching me sputter and try to pull myself together if only for the sake of professionalism. What if some of the messages he was sending all week—the texts, the voice memos, the emails—weren't always serious? Have I let my guard down too much? Has he been flirting with me while I was too busy focused on work to pay attention?

I'm reading too much into this.

But there's no reading too much into that smile. That wicked, knowing smile.

It's a good thing this is going so well because my concentration has hit a wall. All I can think about is that mouth while picking at what's left of my salmon and vegetables. Occasionally, one of the men makes a joke, and I part my lips at the appropriate times.

Otherwise, all I can think about is whether I've made a big mistake in taking this job at all. I don't want him thinking there's anything more to our relationship than business.

I don't want myself thinking about it, either, but it seems like it's too late for me to do anything about that.

"Thank you, gentleman. Truly, it's been a pleasure spending time with you. And I'm glad we could come to an understanding." Sawyer looks my way, maybe waiting for help or any additional niceties, but I'm too tongue-tied for any of that. All I can do is offer a handshake and a smile that I hope is professional and not pained or anxious.

And that leaves the two of us. Well, the two of us along with everybody else in the dining room. They're operating at roughly three-quarter capacity—not terrible, but not great, either. I notice the way Sawyer looks around, the worry lines that seem to magically appear over the bridge of his nose and across his forehead. "You've taken the first step," I assure him in a soft voice. "You sweet talked most of the hardest nuts in town into brushing this off as a misunderstanding. It's going to get better from here."

“I sure as hell hope so.” When he turns my way and meets my gaze, the most unfortunate thing happens. Suddenly, I can't breathe. He has stolen the breath from my lungs. I need to look away but I can't do that, either. There's a thin, invisible tether joining us, demanding I stay rooted to the spot, lost in him.

Code red. Code freaking red. I need to put some miles between us, and now. Otherwise, I could make a big mistake, the kind I wouldn't be able to forgive myself for.

Somehow in the midst of my growing panic, I manage to think clearly. I brought my bag down with me. I have everything I need.

“I should go.” I make a big deal of checking my watch. “I would like to get back to the city at a reasonable time.”

His expression shifts, but the effect lasts only a moment before he nods. “Of course. I don't want to keep you. You've more than earned your fee tonight.”

Bending to pick up my bag from its place beside my chair, I have to laugh at myself. “What did I do? You handled everything so well.”

“Do you want to know a secret?” He grimaces as we begin winding our way through the tables scattered around the room. "I was ready to shit my pants the entire time."

I have to stifle a laugh if only because we're in public. "Charming."

"You know what I mean. I couldn't shake the feeling that I was walking on a thin wire, and things could go either way."

"Nobody would have known. I sure didn't."

"So you think I handled myself well?"

"Would it give you too big a head if I said you did?"

At least he pretends to think it over. "I don't know. It's tough to say. I'm not sure my head could get much bigger."

"No comment." I can't believe I'm actually laughing by the time he holds the front door open for me to step outside.

I needed the fresh air, that much is for sure. A few deep breaths as I walk to the car with Sawyer on my heels goes a long way toward clearing my head. I can handle this. It's not a big deal.

So what if the addition of moonlight and a sky full of stars makes the whole moment entirely too romantic? So what if Sawyer's dark hair gleams in the silvery light that perfectly illuminates his frustratingly chiseled features when we come to a stop? I should stop looking at him, but I can't. And I don't want to.

"Do me a favor?" he asks in a soft voice.

"It depends on the favor," I warn, skeptical.

His head tips to the side. "Have you always possessed this suspicious attitude?"

"Only when it comes to people I'm not sure I can trust."

"Well, I was going to ask you to text me and let me know you got home safely." His lips twitch at my obvious surprise. "What? Not what you were expecting?"

"Frankly, no. It's not."

He takes a tiny step closer, until the toes of our shoes are nearly touching and I am hopelessly overwhelmed thanks to his nearness, to the musky scent of his cologne and the way his gaze keeps darting back and forth between my eyes and my mouth.

"Maybe you need to adjust your opinion of me if it's still so low." Then all at once he's filling the entire world, leaning down to catch my mouth with his before I even know what's happening.

And all at once I grab him by his lapels and clutch them tight, holding him in place while fireworks go off in my head and an absolute inferno flares to life in my core. I can't hear anything over the rush of blood in my ears, the pounding of my heart. We might as well be the only two people in the world, especially once his arms close around my back and he pulls my body flush with his.

It's almost enough to make me forget who's kissing me.

But not quite.

It's the last thing I want to do, pushing him away, but sometimes we have to do the last thing we want if it means recovering our self-respect.

We're both breathing hard, staring at each other. "What is your problem?" he pants. "Don't act like you didn't want me to do that."

"You are so damn full of yourself." It's almost laughable how desperately I need to regain control. Not for him—never for him. For my own sake. So I don't completely lose myself.

"So that wasn't you grabbing me and holding on tight?"

"Don't be such a child." I use the fob on my keychain to unlock the door, then practically throw myself inside before he has the chance to charm me—or worse.

Damn it, Willow. That would have been the worst possible move without factoring in the identity of the client who kissed me. I would beat myself up if he were anybody else, but he isn't anybody else. He is Sawyer Cargill, sentient pond scum.

Sentient pond scum who knows how to kiss. Does he ever.

It was just a kiss, dammit. I can handle a simple kiss.

Maybe if I tell myself so enough times, I'll believe it. Maybe I won't want so much to turn my car around and head straight back to his open arms so he can keep kissing me that way for as long as he wants to.

17

SAWYER

"Am I going to have to pay some of these people off?" I lean back in my chair, sighing, rubbing my temples against an approaching headache.

There's a reason I sent the family helicopter out to Manhattan to pick her up. It's one thing for her to send a snarky comeback via text or to even hear the irritation in a voice memo. But none of that compares to the site of Willow rolling her eyes at yet another one of my deliberately terrible ideas.

"Are you serious?" Before waiting for me to reply, her eyes roll, and that paired with the way she purses her lips—like she tasted something sour—does something to me. I can't help but remember what else those lips do to me.

She remembers, too. It's only Sunday, not even two days since I said *fuck it* and kissed her. I see it in the way she averts her gaze whenever our eyes meet. She doesn't want to look me in the eye, too embarrassed to admit how much she wanted what flared to life between us. No way could she kiss me the way she did without wanting it. The memory threatens to get me as hard as I was in the parking lot, but this isn't the time to indulge the memories. Not when she's seated on the sofa in my office, typing on the MacBook balanced across her lap.

"What?" I ask, because playing dumb makes all of this that much more entertaining. It's too much fun, seeing how far I can push her before she snaps.

"I'm pretty sure it's illegal to pay people off."

"It wouldn't be like that," I protest, stifling a chuckle when she groans.

"Your intention doesn't matter. Bribery is bribery." She pinches the bridge of her nose, sighing. "I swear, I don't know how you managed to get the CEO position at this place."

Before I can say a word, she snaps her fingers. "Of course. Your daddy. How silly of me."

It should infuriate me, this condescending attitude she cops. The way she lowers her brow and all but growls whenever I come up with an admittedly terrible idea. What can I say? I like getting under her skin. That's not the only thing I'd like to get under, come to think of it…

Down, boy. I need to be careful if I don't want to end up being sued for inappropriate behavior or something like that. It's one thing to send her flowers, which have gone unmentioned, or even to text her the way I did yesterday morning to ask if we can have a proper date. She ignored that, too. I have to give her credit for sticking to her guns and being professional. Hell, when I step out of the situation and look at it from an outsider's perspective, I find her resolve admirable.

But as it turns out, her resolve is getting in the way of me getting what I want. Funny how my priorities are muddled now. Yes, I very clearly remember the reason I reached out to her to begin with, but there's no ignoring the tension crackling through the room. How she can pretend the way she does is beyond me.

"Do me a favor and don't talk about my father," I suggest, grimacing at the thought of him. "He is very far away, and I'd prefer to keep it that way. Meaning I don't even want him at the forefront of my thoughts."

She's good, but not good enough to conceal her glee. "I thought he was the entire reason we were doing this."

"That doesn't mean I want to think about him if I can avoid it."

"Fair enough." Though she's still grinning to herself when she pulls out her legal pad and checks her notes.

While she's distracted, I have no choice but to indulge in every inch of her. It's a Sunday, and it's just the two of us, so neither of us is in our usual business attire. She wears a modest dress with ruffled sleeves that match the ruffles along the hem which grazes the middle of her calves. Rather than her mile-high stilettos, she wears a pair of flats, and her hair is pulled back in a simple, low ponytail.

In other words, it seems like she's trying to play down her looks. Minimal makeup, little jewelry. What is she trying to do? Not turn me on? That's about as likely right now as me learning to breathe underwater. No, if anything, I can appreciate her natural beauty without the designer labels getting in the way.

Hunger stirs as I watch her tap her pen against her bottom lip. Every once in a while she catches the cap between her teeth—I don't know why the action leaves me breathless, glued to her every move.

Somehow I force myself to pull it together when she looks my way once again. "So what else do we have on the agenda today?" I ask, clearing my throat and sitting up a bit straighter. She wants to pretend the kiss never happened, and I have no choice but to play along if only for now. Until I catch her in the right mood again, anyway.

"There are still a few people who won't budge," she says with a sigh. "Not city council, but people who have pull in the community. A couple of them are on your board, in fact. And if they're still pissed at you and don't want you as CEO..."

"They'll bend the council's ear," I conclude with a groan. Just like that, all thoughts of her enticing perfume are wiped away.

"We need to get those people on your side."

"You make it sound so simple."

"I have my ways."

I arch an eyebrow. The woman knows how to get my attention. "Enlighten me."

"For one thing, one of the men has a gambling problem."

Now both eyebrows shoot straight up. “Who?”

“Not so fast, hot shot. I don't blab information like that so easily.”

“But this is important.”

“Sure it is, but that doesn't mean I'm going to air somebody else's dirty laundry. Suffice it to say, I have ways of getting through to people who would rather keep their vices quiet.”

“I appreciate your ethics, but this is sounding a lot like blackmail.”

“Not at all,” she insists, blithe, almost carefree. “There are diplomatic ways to let someone know you're onto them, and if they'd rather keep their private drama to themselves, they should learn to play along. And maybe if they don't, their growing gambling debt might be of interest to the rest of the board.”

“Why do I feel like you shouldn't tell me anymore?”

Her lips twitch with humor. “Plausible deniability. One of the first solid moves you've made recently.”

“Excuse me, but I did just fine on Friday.”

Her cheeks flush, but she nods. "Yes, you did very well." It is so tempting, the impulse to push a little harder, to bring up the kiss. It's obvious she's thinking about it, or why else would she blush?

Instead, I take the high road. "Do you have anything else on the outliers?"

"Actually, yes. Nathan Fields likes to pretend he's committed to green living, but he drives a vintage car on the weekends and is even part of a club where they show off their gas guzzlers. Rob Myers is in the same club."

"Oh, yeah. I have no doubt."

"So, it only makes sense that he would use that connection to plant ideas in Rob's head. But don't worry about that, either. I'll have my people reach out to him to discuss his hypocrisy."

It isn't so much what she says, but the way she says it. I have the feeling she would make an absolutely bloodthirsty general, leading her troops into battle.

"Good. I like a woman who's… thorough," I manage, my tongue tripping over the word. Probably because the image in my head is one of a warrior, weapons drawn, screaming at her troops to charge.

Besides, the only other word that came to mind was *dominant*, and I don't know if that would be safe to use. It might take the conversation in an unfortunate direction.

"That's me to a T." Her tone is light, almost distracted, but she's not fooling me. This straightening of her shoulders and slight lifting of her chin tell a different story. She appreciates the praise.

"Unlike you," she's quick to add. "You can't even keep your mouth shut in public."

Ahh, yes. The inevitable one-two punch. She can't let our interaction become too friendly. There's always a dig waiting in the wings.

"That has nothing to do with thoroughness. I can be very thorough under the right circumstances."

She only snorts, turning her attention back to her computer. "I'm sure you can."

"Exceptionally thorough."

"I am not arguing with you."

No, but she's not looking at me, either. I need her to look at me. I realize it makes me nothing more than a spoiled child demanding attention, but so be it. I want her attention.

I could get it, too. I could explain how thoroughly I would ravish her here and now if the situation were different. If she would just open up and let me in. No pun intended, but that would help, too. I could show her there are better ways to spend a Sunday than cooped up in an office, both of us fully dressed, talking over strategies. I could take her here on this desk, stretch her out in front of me and go to town on that luscious body. The thought leaves me breathless, my heart racing, my jaw clenched as I wrestle with the lust I can't seem to control.

"You drive me crazy, you know that?" I ask, grinning in spite of myself.

"The feeling's mutual, Sawyer." Her gaze never leaves her screen. Always business, this one.

It's clear I need to find a way to mix business with pleasure. I came close on Friday night. She revealed how eager she is to explore the undeniable attraction between us. How easy it is to stoke the fire burning under the surface.

I can do that again. I need to do that again.

And next time, I am not going to back down so easily.

18

WILLOW

"How did it get so late?"

I look up from the press release I've been fooling with, shocked to find the sky outside the window completely dark. "Oh, my God," I murmur, laughing. "I had no idea."

Sawyer chuckles before slowly unfolding his body from his leather chair. "You're a lot like me."

"And how is that, exactly?" I ask, suspicious.

He groans, shaking his head. "You don't have to sound like I just insulted you, you know."

"I didn't."

"You kind of did." He smirks while stretching, twisting from one side to the other before stretching his arms over his head.

Arms now only partially covered thanks to the polo shirt he's wearing. I've never seen him dressed so casually, and I sincerely wish the sight of his forearms wasn't so enticing. What is it about a pair of well sculpted forearms that turns me to jelly? They're tan, too, thick, strong.

And here I am, biting my lip so hard I might break the skin.

"Are you hungry?" Somehow, he manages to make an innocent question sound anything but. Or maybe that's my immature, out-of-control lust playing tricks on me.

Though he raises a good point. "Starving," I admit with a sheepish grin. "Sometimes, I lose track of everything else when I'm working."

"Which is what I meant, by the way, before you got insulted."

"I did not get insulted."

"So you say. Honestly, this would all be a lot easier if you would just be honest with me. You always have to treat everything like we're in battle."

Maybe I wouldn't have to if you hadn't scarred me psychologically. The retort is on the tip of my tongue, ready to spill out of my mouth, but I pull back at the last second. We won't get anywhere if this devolves into a full-out fight.

"I guess I've never reacted well to being teased."

His features pinch like I've wounded him—or like a memory has. "Point taken. I was going to suggest we order dinner from downstairs if you'd be interested. The kitchen will still be open for another half hour."

I should say no, shouldn't I? I should make up an excuse about having to go home. We've already spent too much time together today—there was no need for me to come in, but he insisted and even added that damn helicopter to boot. Wealthy people can do things like that. And here I am, playing into it, the way I always swore I wouldn't.

Though I can't pretend it wasn't sort of cool, being whisked away in a helicopter at a moment's notice. The sort of thing I might be able to get used to and even enjoy once I get over the absolutely terrifying sensation of floating in a tin can.

He's waiting, expectant. "I don't know..." *Just say no, you idiot. Tell him you have things to do and ask if you can take the helicopter back.*

"You're considering turning down a free dinner?"

"You're the one paying me all this money. I can afford to buy dinner somewhere else."

"Touché. But come on. Don't act like you didn't love that salmon you had on Friday. You practically licked the plate."

"I did not!"

"Sure, if it makes you feel better. You didn't."

"Oh, shut up." But damn it, a giggle slips out before I can help it. He has a way of getting to me. I can't pretend otherwise.

"I thought you didn't like being teased."

I'm actually glad he said it, the jerk. "See? There you go again. You never know when to let up. Always needing to take that extra step, to push just a little harder. And it's that impulse that's landed us here."

"And there you go. Always dropping a lesson."

Am I being ridiculous? It's just dinner. And I am very hungry—to the point where I would have to stop off and grab something to eat before trying to make it home. "Fine. If you're willing to have dinner, I guess I could eat, too."

"Very big of you."

He is such a dick. I have to bite my tongue to keep my thoughts to myself. It's safer to turn my attention back to the press release. I'll have Sarah look it over for me, since we always act as the other's second pair of eyes when it comes to things like this. I would never go public with a release without letting her pick it apart first.

As it is, it looks pretty good. We've discussed the idea of starting a charity or a fund to highlight Sawyer's commitment to the community at large, and I think I've landed on something in his wheelhouse.

After a conversation with someone working downstairs, Sawyer hangs up the phone wearing what looks like a satisfied table grin. “What's up?”

“We came in at ninety percent capacity tonight.” He turns away quickly, looking out the window, but not fast enough to conceal the gratified smile that lights up his face. He wants to hide it from me, but I'm watching him too closely.

You shouldn't watch him like that. I really wish that voice in my head would shut up sometimes. It's my job to watch him closely, to read his moods, to anticipate his stupid, reckless ideas.

Sure. Keep telling yourself that.

"I'm happy to hear it," I murmur, studying him, observing the way his hands tighten into fists once they're deep in the pockets of his khakis. The way his broad shoulders rise and fall when he sighs. He is much more emotionally attached to the outcome of this situation than he ever meant to let on. He wants so badly to right the wrongs he unwittingly committed.

Dear God. I am actually defending him to myself. Sawyer fucking Cargill, the devil incarnate.

It's even worse than that. I'm not only defending him. I am sympathizing with him.

"I have big plans for this place," he admits, still facing the harbor. "I can see it all in my head. Making it bigger and better than anything my father ever imagined. I'm not talking about some sprawling monolith, either."

"So you mean what you say about wanting the club to be the heart of the town?"

"I don't necessarily think of it in those terms—but yes. In a way. I want this club to be what immediately comes to mind when someone is planning an event. I want happy memories to be made here—not only private dinners and drinks after sailing, but something people remember for years to come."

And here I sit, waiting for the punchline. Expecting him to say something awful, or selfish, or egotistical.

No such thing happens. I don't know if I'm surprised or secretly glad. "I commend you for that."

"I didn't say it to be commended."

"Can you take a compliment when it's offered? I swear, that's the exact sort of thing you got on my case for, a couple of days ago."

"And there I was, thinking you forgot all about Friday's events."

Whoops. There it is. The exact sort of ignorant, egotistical statement I was expecting. He would have to throw that in my face, wouldn't he? I'm not going to give him the satisfaction of playing into his hand.

Besides, our dinner has arrived.

"So, what do you do in your free time?" he asks while slicing into a succulent filet whose aroma sort of makes me wish I'd ordered that, instead. He likes it medium rare, too, which is exactly how I always order my beef. It's a shame we're not friendly, or I would ask for a bite.

"Free time? What's that?"

"Same here," he agrees with a sigh. "There are people who treat work like work, and then there are those of us who can't draw the line between work and life. This club is my life."

It takes a second for me to understand he's being sincere. And for some reason, I feel sorry for him. "You're too young to lock yourself away in a yacht club for the rest of your life."

"And how is the view from up on your high horse?" he counters, but not without humor. "You know what I mean. My work weaves itself into my life. If I'm socializing, it's here. Having drinks at the club. Eating dinner?"

The pointed look he gives his plate makes me laugh. "Gotcha."

"Don't tell me you're not the same way."

"I am. I won't argue with you. The only thing I've taken to bed in as long as I can remember is my computer."

Wow. Where the hell did that come from? Like he needs to know anything about my private life and the fact that I haven't gotten laid in far too long.

He coughs softly like he's dislodging food from his throat. "That is a pity."

I need this meal to be over. I need this day to be over. I should have gone home when I had the chance. The fact is, the more time I spend with him, the more dangerous this whole situation becomes. But I can't pretend he's not charming, and that it isn't easy to forget why I wanted to turn him down in the first place. What is it about him that makes me so eager to forget all the hurt he caused me?

By the time we finish eating, it's past ten o'clock. Not exactly shockingly late, but late enough after a long day of work that my eyes are burning from the exertion of staring at my screen all day. My body's in knots, too. My muscles are stiff. "Remind me to invoice you for the massage I'll need after all this sitting around in one place."

I almost swallow my tongue when I realize what I just said, but he takes the high road instead of offering me a complimentary rubdown. "By all means. Feel free."

He then checks his watch, frowning. "I kept you here way too late. Honestly, I apologize."

"No need." I start gathering my things, placing them in my bag.

"There's a problem, though. I'm not sure I can request the helicopter this late. I mean, I can, but it's sort of a dick move at this time of night."

"If I didn't know better, I'd think you kept me here this late on purpose."

"I didn't, I swear." He holds up a hand, then makes a cross over his chest with his forefinger.

"It's alright. I can afford a cab back to town."

"You could also stay here."

"Here?" I look around, snickering. "I mean, do you really want me sleeping on your leather couch?"

"I meant you could take a room at our hotel. It's not a busy night at the club, there should be at least one room available."

I should probably turn him down, but I'm too tired to do anything but agree. All I want is to close my eyes in a comfortable bed. "Sure. Thanks. I can always go back tomorrow."

"Excellent. Come on. I'll walk you down. You need a special key to access those floors."

On the way down, goosebumps pebble my skin when it occurs to me that Sawyer Cargill is walking me to my hotel room. Where there will obviously be a bed. Was this all part of his master plan? Maybe I need to stop being so suspicious, but then there's a good reason for it. I can't trust him.

You can't trust the little boy he used to be. He's not that boy anymore, just like you are not that girl.

I can't believe how much I want that to be true as we step off the elevator and emerge in a tasteful, softly lit hallway. Unlike the strong, masculine feel of the executive floor, this is much calmer. Inviting. I could easily be in the hallway of someone's home. Someone's extremely expensive home.

"Here we go. Our best room, complete with a stunning view." He opens the door for me, then sweeps an arm to usher me inside. Immediately, my attention is drawn to the floor-to-ceiling windows which do indeed allow for a breathtaking view of the harbor. There are boats out there, even at this time of night, some of them strung with white twinkle lights that reflect off the water and create a dreamy look. The slightly waning moon casts silvery light caught by countless tiny ripples.

"It's really beautiful," I murmur, my breath catching as I drink in the scene.

He stands behind me, alarmingly close. The scent of his cologne threatens to undo the last of my weakening resolve. "Yes. It is."

This is becoming an entirely too intimate moment. I leave my bag on the coffee table and sink onto a white linen sofa. "I should have the press release finished by the end of the day tomorrow. I'll send it over to you for final approval once I'm satisfied with it."

"Do you ever think of anything but your work?"

"I would think you'd be grateful for that. Remember, this is all for you."

"It just strikes me as sort of sad that you would step into a room like this and immediately turn to work."

I'm doing it because it's safer than getting personal. "Just a habit, I guess. But I've been thinking seriously about one of the ideas we discussed to earn the trust and respect of your neighbors; a nonprofit run by the Somerset Yacht Club."

His mouth twists in a smirk that does not bode well. "The sailing school idea?"

"Sure. A chance for underprivileged kids to learn to sail, to spend time out on the water during the summer. These kids would never get that opportunity otherwise. It would be a really great gesture, especially if you opened it here, on the grounds of the club."

"It would take a lot of work."

"Most things do," I remind him, kicking off my flats. "But it would earn you a ton of good will."

"I would have to run it by the board, of course."

"You can do that once the press release is approved. I won't release it until they give the okay."

"I don't know if they will."

"Well, maybe you should offer a public apology, after all. Like you first suggested. That way, the board will know you're serious, that you're dedicated to making things right. That could go a long way towards softening them on the idea, and on you."

"Hold on a second." He sits beside me—way too close for comfort, in fact, and my shoulders immediately rise up around my ears at his nearness.

At the same time, a familiar heat spreads through my core, heating my skin and tightening my nipples, making my heart race and my breathing quicken. I need to learn how to control myself at moments like this—he's just a man, a man like any other. I can handle him.

"Is there a problem with that idea?" I ask rather than focus on the telltale aching between my thighs.

"I thought you were against the idea of a public apology."

"I was, but now that we have a better idea of how people feel—"

"So now, after everything else you've put me through, you expect me to eat crow in public. It's not enough I had to host those blowhards from the city council and basically prostrate myself in front of them?"

"For once, would you put your ego aside?"

"For once, would you stop asking me to do the impossible?" He suddenly bolts up from the couch and begins pacing in front of the window. "First you say no public apology and treat me like an asshole for even suggesting it, and now you act like it's your big idea and I should thank you for it."

"When did I ever say you should thank me for it?"

"You're the one who didn't want to draw further attention to the video."

"Would you please take a breath?" Even for him, this is completely startling. He's a pain in the ass, but he's usually reasonable enough not to jump to these outrageous conclusions.

"Don't tell me to take a breath," he snarls. "I'm sick to death of being confused by you. Make up your mind, woman."

And now I'm starting to wonder if we are actually arguing about a public apology.

"I told you at the beginning that you'd have to do everything I say, no argument." I stand, hands on my hips, and suddenly my exhaustion fades away, replaced by outrage. "Sometimes we have to change course based on the way things are going. It was not the right move at first, but now that I have a better idea of what we're dealing with, you might need to make an apology to close the deal. Why is that so difficult for you to understand?"

"Because I'm sick to death of feeling like I have no control over this situation, damn it."

"By all means. Take that out on me. You know, the only person who can actually help you."

"There you go again, on your high horse."

"Says the man willing to offer me four hundred grand to get the job done," I fire back.

"We can end this right here and now, if you'd rather." He folds his arms, stepping up to me while wearing his patented know-it-all smirk. "What do you think about that?"

I mimic his posture, staring him straight in the eye. "I think you're too much of a coward to say you're sorry in public, so you would rather shoot yourself in the foot by firing me."

"Oh, yeah?"

"Yes. That's exactly what I think."

"Do you know what I think?"

Before I can tell him I don't give a fuck, he takes my face in his hands and crushes his lips against mine.

19

SAWYER

Could this be the biggest mistake I've ever made, kissing her, finally breaking the unbearable tension? I could be accused of doing this to shut her up, but that wouldn't be true. No, this is what I want. This is what I've always wanted. To hold her, to touch, and kiss, and taste, and explore. To feel.

This time, she doesn't fight me off right away. Her tongue slides past mine, in fact, lighting up every nerve in my body and making me sizzle from head to toe. How did she do this to me? How does she know exactly what I need, how I need it? Because I need her to kiss me like she is now, with all the heat and passion I knew simmered beneath the surface all this time. I need her nails digging into my shoulders—damn it, I'm wearing too much clothing, we both are. I want her skin, I need her hands on me.

It's when I begin pulling my polo from my waistband that the moment shatters and Willow backs away, shaking her head furiously before bumping into the sofa and falling back on it in a flushed, breathless heap. “No. That is not happening.”

“What are you saying? Don't pretend you didn't—”

“Okay, so I was into it, but one of us has to be smart and it's got to be me. I will not let you do this to me.”

I can’t help but show the intense frustration that now battles with unquenched thirst. “Damn it, what do you think I'm trying to do to you?”

“How can you expect me to trust you after everything? What, I'm supposed to forget how we started out?”

Right now, with my dick screaming to be free and my entire body screaming for release, every impulse leaves me wanting to brush her off, to tell her it doesn't matter. That was the past, we were different people, all of that.

But there are more important things than getting off—which I very much need to do.

Yet instead of charging the sofa and pinning her with my body, I slowly lower myself beside her. Her shoulders hunch and she folds her arms, and that's my fault. I can accept that.

"Look at me." When she doesn't right away, I take the chance of reaching over and hooking a finger beneath her chin, turning her head. Stubborn thing—she still tries to fight it, but I'm too persistent.

"I'm sorry. I am so sorry for what I did to you." I lean in, gratified when she doesn't pull away, and this time the brush of our mouths is soft but no less electric. No, if anything, that slight touch leaves me panting for more.

"Just saying it isn't good enough. I'm sorry, but that's how it is."

Another kiss, another, and she can't silence the soft sighs each touch of my lips stirs up.

"Do you want to know the truth?" I whisper before kissing her again, this time on one flushed, downy cheek. "Boarding school was a miserable experience." I slide my lips along her jawline, noting the goosebumps pebbling her neck and shoulder as I continue caressing her. "I had no choice whether I wanted to attend. I felt abandoned, rejected."

"You sure didn't seem that way."

"Haven't you ever heard of coping mechanisms?" God, her skin is magic, and I want to taste every inch of it. "No matter what I did, it wasn't good enough. If I got an A, why wasn't it an A plus? If I made co-captain of the basketball team, why wasn't I the solo captain? Nothing I did was ever up to his standards. I was completely cut off from everybody and everything I knew. And I was stupid enough to take that out on others. Including you."

When our eyes meet this time, I find hers hazy with a mixture of lust and understanding. The lust is gratifying, but it's the understanding I need. That's all that matters right now, because if this is going anywhere, she needs to forgive me.

"I'm not that stupid little boy anymore." She is so impossibly soft, her cheek like silk beneath my fingers as I stroke from temple to chin. She leans into my touch and my heart soars. "Can you ever forgive me?" I whisper with my heart in my throat.

"You wouldn't be saying all of this just to get into my panties, would you?"

I can't help chuckling. Even now, she has to be a hard ass. "You know, the fact that you would ask that probably plays a large part in why it's been so important for me to get through to you. You don't take any shit, but that only means working harder to get you to trust me. That's all I want. For you to trust me. I'm no good at any of this," I have to admit. "I have never fought like this for a woman. I never thought it was necessary. I've never been the settling down type or even the boyfriend type, but you?"

My fingers travel the slim column of her throat before dancing along her collarbone until she shivers. "You have me feeling things I didn't think were possible, not for me."

She places her hand over mine, holding it still before taking a deep breath. "This isn't just another bullshit apology like the one you gave me at the dance, is it? You aren't going to pull the rug out from under me again, right?"

I hate that she has to ask that. "I will never do that to you again. You have my word, Willow. Hell, you have all of me."

To prove it, I slide from the couch to the floor, lowering myself to my knees in front of her. "This is where you have me. Absolutely humbled by your beauty and your intelligence and your absolute determination to put me through my paces. All I want is a chance to prove how sincere I am when I say I want you. All of you."

She jumps slightly when my hands land on her knees but doesn't push me away, instead she sighs as I slowly spread her thighs. I can hardly breathe as I inch the hem of her dress up her legs, exposing more and more of her to me before running my mouth over the ultra-smooth, soft skin of her inner thighs. She slides down until her delectable ass is at the edge of the cushion and I take advantage, hooking my fingers around the waistband of her lacy panties and slowly working them down, tantalizing both of us in the process. By the time they're around her ankles I'm practically salivating, so eager to worship her as she deserves.

"You are so beautiful," I whisper before lowering my head, running my tongue along her glistening seam and picking up the taste of the excitement that coats her lips. I can't help but groan as my desire explodes into something all-consuming. Something so powerful there's no hope of fighting it.

And she feels it, too. She must, or else why would she moan the way she does while her fingers tangle in my hair? "Just like that," she groans, suddenly grasping my head tighter, holding it in place while my tongue works her wet, swollen folds. "Yes. Harder. I want you to eat me, Sawyer."

Dear God. I'm about a heartbeat away from finishing in my pants by the time I release a growl and do as the lady asks. I eat her like a man starved, like only the taste of her sweet nectar will satisfy my hunger. Focusing on her pink bud I wrap my lips around it and suck, flicking the tip with my tongue, and she rewards me by raking her nails over my arms and grinding against my face.

"So good... feels so good... oh, god, yes Sawyer..." Her body undulates like a wave, passion finally overtaking her and turning her into something feral. A look up at her reveals a woman drowning in lust: eyes closed, mouth hanging open, her head rolling back and forth while one guttural moan after another fills the air.

I had no idea until now that's exactly what I want, what I need. It leaves me sucking harder, following her commands, eager to please her. Desperate to tease out an orgasm—one of many I plan to give her.

"Sawyer... Sawyer, yes... make me come... I'm going to...!" And then she comes undone, her hips jerking upward, thighs closing tight around my head, blocking out everything but the sound of blood rushing in my ears as she rides the wave before eventually crashing down, breathless, trembling.

I knew it would be good. I never imagined it would be this good. That I would feel this powerful, this triumphant as I raise my head.

Or that she would immediately sit up, her greedy hands plucking at my clothes in a frenzied effort to strip me down. There's no holding back a surprised laugh at her eagerness, but then I'm eager, too. Especially once I pull the polo over my head and her electric touch against my bare skin sends a jolt of pure pleasure racing through me.

Somehow I manage to lower the zipper at the back of her dress and she lets it fall away from her upper body, revealing a pair of creamy breasts that almost overflow their bra cups with every deep, ragged breath. Her head falls back when I bury my face between them, lapping at her skin, working my tongue beneath the satin to swipe it across her nipples.

She reaches behind her to unclasp the hooks, leaving me to feast on her bare flesh until she falls against me, knocking me on my back so she can straddle my hips.

Our eyes meet an instant before she lifts the dress over her head and tosses it aside along with the elastic holding her hair back. The sight of her takes my breath away—she's a goddess, nothing short of that, and the hunger blazing in her hazel eyes tells me we are far from finished with what we started.

She falls forward, palms against my chest, and practically devours my mouth while grinding against my painfully erect dick. I manage to work the belt and zipper, shoving the khakis down along with my shorts and finally springing free.

"Do you have protection?" she whispers between kisses against my chest, my abs, while her hands roam every bare inch of skin. It takes a little work now that nearly all the blood in my head has rushed south, but I manage to fish my wallet out of my pants to remove the condom tucked inside.

Her hands shake as she unrolls the latex down my thick shaft, and once it's ready she hovers over me, prepared to direct me to her quivering entrance. It never occurs to me to take control. I'd rather watch her take what she needs. It's a thrill I've never known and I want to savor every moment of it.

We both groan when she lowers herself, allowing me inside her tight heat. "Fuck..." she sighs, her eyes closing, her head falling back, while all I can do is grit my teeth and hang on because there's nothing I want more than to let go once her still fluttering muscles begin massaging me.

"Ride me." With a growl, I take hold of her hips, digging my fingers into her firm flesh before she begins rocking back and forth. Every downstroke leaves her grinding against my base, her soft cries of pleasure getting louder, louder.

"Oh, my God… so big…" she whines, bracing her palms against my chest before quickening her pace.

"Take what you want," I growl through gritted teeth. "Fuck me. Make yourself come on my cock, baby."

"Sawyer…!" Her muscles begin tightening, gripping me until I see stars. The familiar tingle begins at the base of my spine and I know I can't hold on much longer. When she cries out once more, loud and throaty, tightness turns to the fluttering and massaging of her muscles drawing me deeper, milking my shaft until I have no choice but to explode in a rush of release.

By the time I come to, when the ringing in my ears subsides and reality comes drifting back through the fading haze, her body is stretched out across mine—and she's softly chuckling.

"If I thought it would be that good," she whispers, "we would've done that before now."

"We clearly have a lot of lost time to make up for." And as far as I'm concerned, we have all night.

Hell, we have the rest of our lives.

20

WILLOW

There's something lying across my chest.

For some reason, that's the first conscious thought that crosses my mind before I open my eyes, blinking away the harsh sunlight coming from the window beside the bed. Somehow, we made it to the bed last night—and the sheets tangled around my damp body reflect what took place once we got here.

It's Sawyer's arm on my chest, and he's beside me, lying on his stomach with his face turned away from mine. He's just as spent as I am after three rounds—or was it 4? I sort of lost track. There's only one thing I know for sure: I have never felt so free to say and do exactly what I wanted, needed. I have never come so hard, either, to the point where I was afraid something broke inside me. I just couldn't stop. It was almost too intense, even scary.

But I was in his arms. And I trusted him. I trust this man, finally.

Now, it's me I'm concerned with. It's me I can't trust.

I squeeze my eyes shut, willing away my worries. I am not going to ruin this moment by second guessing everything. Instead, I take a deep breath, savoring the lingering scent of Sawyer's cologne. It's all over me, on my skin and in my hair. I'm limp with exhaustion, but the best kind. The kind that makes me smile while my cheeks flush and my heart races.

Even though he's my client.

There I go again, and this time there's a pit in my stomach that begins to grow. This is the least professional thing I could have done, no matter how much I wanted it. No matter how good it feels to know I finally conquered Sawyer Cargill, that he apologized for everything he did and even opened himself up to me and explained why, that doesn't erase the fact that I broke the one cardinal rule of business. You don't sleep with a client, a partner, anybody you're doing business with.

My pleasure is fading, replaced by massive, crushing guilt much heavier than the tanned arm rising and falling with my every breath. How am I supposed to enjoy this when I can't stop berating myself for giving in? It doesn't matter how much I wanted it. I want a lot of things. And the fresh batteries I bought last week should have been enough to satisfy my constant craving for him.

No, a vibrator is no replacement for the man lying beside me, I know that for sure now. But it should have been enough. I should have made it enough.

Even if he feels like what's been missing from my life all this time. The missing piece of my puzzle. This isn't just a matter of afterglow screwing with my head. There's so much more to us than the sex alone, which is what makes the sex as good as it is. He gets me. I get him. Even when we're at each other's throats, there's something undeniable that sprang up the second we set eyes on each other in his office.

And when I turn my head to look at him again, I find him smiling at me. He's drowsy, but there's no mistaking the satisfaction in his grin. My entire body shouldn't go warm the way it does. My heart shouldn't swell. Yet here I am.

"Hi." His voice is still thick with sleep, but it's warm. I might even say happy.

"Hi," I whisper back as I begin stroking his forearm. "Good morning."

"It's Monday."

"I know."

"I guess that means we should get up?"

I pretend to think about it, but there's no denying that getting out of this bed and going back to Manhattan is the last thing I want to do. "First, we should get a shower," I reason, pretending to be serious. "Then, we should eat breakfast. I'm famished thanks to all the exertion you put me through."

"Don't expect me to apologize."

"I wouldn't." I pause, grinning. "Then, I think we should go for Round Two. Or is it Round Five?"

His sly, knowing grin makes my stomach flip flop. "I've lost count, but that sounds like a good idea to me. I'll make coffee while you get in the shower. What do you want to eat?" He rolls away from me to pick up the phone on his side of the bed.

"I can eat just about anything. Eggs, pancakes, waffles—whatever you think the kitchen does best." I would really rather he join me in the shower, but let's face it, we won't get very far without any food in our stomachs.

It's like all the contention that used to exist between us has turned to warmth, intimacy, and I can't help but sneak glimpses of him while we eat, both of us sitting cross legged in the bed, wearing plush robes provided by the hotel. They really did think of everything, and the luxury surrounding us only adds to the sense of existing in some special world that belongs only to the two of us.

He decided to go with a little bit of everything, and I'm glad of that when I polish off my half of a waffle paired with scrambled eggs and crisp bacon. "This is heaven. What's the thread count on these sheets?"

His lips stir while he lifts his coffee cup. "I don't have the first clue. You like them?"

"They're the softest sheets I've ever slept on."

"What about other activities?" Before I know it, he's setting our plates on the tray and placing it on the nightstand.

Then he lunges for me. "I just ate!" I squeal.

"We need to work off some of those calories." He's already tugging at the belt of my robe, opening it, exploring me with hands, and lips, and tongue.

"I'm not the one who ate four pieces of bacon and a pile of home fries."

He lifts his head just long enough to wink and retort, "Then I'll have to do all the work."

I wouldn't stop him if I could, because already I'm wet again, aching, like my body has a mind of its own. He settles between my legs and I wrap them around his hips, sighing in contentment when he kisses me deeply. I can't imagine ever getting tired of touching him, letting my hands roam under his robe until I slide them over his shoulders. His broad, muscular shoulders, just as muscular as the arms caging me against his firm, warm body.

We aren't even fully undressed before there's a familiar and welcome pressure between my thighs. It was during a brief break in the evening's activities that we discussed our histories. We're both disease free and I'm on the pill, so there's no stopping for a condom this time.

"My God," I groan as he pushes forward, filling me again, stretching me with his thick member.

He claims my mouth with his, our tongues dancing, the delicious friction building with every stroke. I moan into his mouth and he groans back, the sound a rumble in his chest that only heightens my excitement. He wants this as much as I do. I have what it takes to please him, to light his fire, to satisfy him. Me. He wants me.

He breaks the kiss, gazing down at me while rolling his hips and deepening his stroke. "Oh, yeah," I groan, moving with him. "Just like that. I want to feel every inch of you."

"I think I died and went to heaven." He closes his eyes, his jaw going tight, and I drink in his beauty. The morning sunlight plays off his skin until it glows, highlighting his chiseled face until it makes my chest hurt to look at him. What is happening to me? What's already happened?

The source of the growing tension in my core is easier to identify. "So big," I whisper. "Fuck me harder, Sawyer. Make me come again." My nails drag down his back, drawing a hiss of pain that quickly turns to a guttural moan.

And a flurry of deep, almost brutal thrusts that leave me helpless, writhing and panting until the tension is too much. Until an explosion goes off deep inside that sends ripples of pleasure shooting through me and there's nothing to do but shout. "Yes! Yes!"

"So tight…" I can barely hear him even when he growls it close to my ear. "So fucking tight… Willow… oh, fuck…!" A rush of warmth paired with his deep grunts make me smile even while I shudder in release. There's a satisfaction that goes beyond the physical. Something like pride, I guess. I do this to him. He's able to lose himself in me, to be totally vulnerable.

I can't lose myself in him.

He collapses for a second but is quick to push himself up on his palms. He's wearing a soft, drowsy sort of smile and I'll be damned if I haven't already lost myself. At least, that's what the butterflies in my stomach are telling me.

I know who this man is. I know what he's like and can guess how he feels about commitment. This can't be more than sex.

No matter how much it feels like it is.

21

SAWYER

"You know, we're going to have to go back to real life soon."

Willow lifts her head from my chest, and I brush a strand of hair from her eyes before nodding in grim acceptance of her unsolicited reminder. "I know. But not this very minute, right?"

"Right." When she rests her head again, it's with a soft sigh I'm not sure I was supposed to hear.

I turn my gaze back out toward the marina beyond the window. I know it like the back of my own hand after spending most of my life with it spread out before me. Farther west, inland, sits a portion of the town, and now that darkness has begun to fall there's the glimmer of light from windows here and there. So many people going about their usual Monday routine while the two of us shut the world out.

But it's like an elephant in the room that only grows larger with every tick of the clock. The closer we get to the inevitable parting, the more painfully obvious it becomes, there is a very important, possibly uncomfortable, discussion in the near future.

I might have completely ruined my chances of sitting comfortably, securely in the chair in the CEO's office. The fact is, if Willow ends up being unhappy by the time we leave this hotel room, there's a solid possibility this could all go up in smoke. All the hard work she's put in, the work I've put in, could be for nothing if this ends badly. Never in my life have I been so acutely aware of my every word, my every decision. I can't hurt her —but I'm not sure there's any way out of this where she doesn't get hurt.

I'm not the relationship type. I don't have the time. Not with the yacht club needing my constant attention. It wouldn't be fair to her—to say nothing of the life she leads, a life miles away from here. I couldn't ask her to give that up for the sake of being with me, and I can't leave. This is where my life is.

It's impossible from every angle. There is simply no way for this to work out.

All this circular thinking is beginning to pick my brain to pieces. I can't even enjoy the welcome weight of Willow's body curled up against mine. She is so effortlessly sexy in her robe, pulled down over her tucked up legs until she's almost fully covered.

Something stirs in my chest and I want nothing more than to wrap her in my arms and hold her close. She's strong, yes, and brilliant. But she's also small, and beneath that tough as nails exterior there's someone soft and vulnerable. The fact that I want to shield her from the world when I caused her so much pain years ago is just one more of life's unpredictable twists. Here I am, wanting to protect her, when I'm probably part of the reason that hard exterior exists now.

Is she going to regret letting that exterior fall away?

A brief knock on the door startles us both, and she's quicker than I am to jump up. "Thank God. I'm starving," she murmurs, belting her robe tighter on her way to accept our dinner order. I can't help but check out her ass as she hustles across the room. How it's possible for my dick to stir after all the work I've put it through in less than twenty-four hours is a mystery. I'm a healthy man who hasn't yet hit the age of thirty, but everybody has their limits. Maybe the limits don't matter when there's a woman like Willow involved.

I'm becoming a hopeless sap, in other words.

Once she begins to swing the door open, Willow offers a single word. "Oh."

That's all she has the chance to say before the door swings open fully and a familiar voice rings out. "You had better have a damn good explanation for being shacked up with yet another strange woman while the fate of my club hangs in the balance."

At first, my brain can't catch up with what's happening. It's all too surreal. Did I fall asleep somehow? Am I dreaming this? Because surely, only in the worst nightmare would my father suddenly appear out of nowhere when he's supposed to be thousands of miles from here.

"Dad." No, the floor feels solid beneath my feet when I stand, and the once soft, luxurious robe now feels scratchy against my icy skin. This is real. My father, practically my mirror image, is glaring at me from the center of the room while Willow stands open mouthed, frozen in shock with the door still hanging open.

"You." He glances over his shoulder, snorting derisively. "Make yourself busy someplace else. I need to talk with my son."

From the corner of my eye I catch sight of her embarrassed flush. "No, don't talk to her that way," I quickly insist.

He swings around, and the wrinkles around his eyes deepen when he blurts out a disbelieving laugh. "What, is she *The One*? Am I supposed to respect your latest conquest?"

Willow's sharp gasp is a knife in my chest. "She is not a conquest," I grit out. "You don't have the first idea what you're talking about."

"Yes, I'm sure." Looking me up and down, he folds his arms. I can't help but notice the fresh tan he sports. He must have been enjoying his trip before coming back unannounced.

"Fine," he continues. "She can stick around if you don't mind being embarrassed in front of her. Because if you don't think I'm going to speak my mind after learning about that damn video and the fact that we are going to lose the city council vote because of it, you have another think coming."

"We are not going to lose the vote. Maybe if you had, I don't know, made a simple phone call, you wouldn't have needed to take the trouble of coming back. I could have told you Willow here is helping me deal with the situation."

"Oh, yes," he mutters with a smirk. "It looks like she's helping you quite a bit. I see we've kept this business meeting extremely casual."

"Excuse me." Willow's whisper is barely audible before she darts into the bathroom and closes, then locks the door. The urge to go after her is almost too much to resist, but she doesn't need to witness this if she doesn't want to. I'm afraid all I would do is hurt her, anyway, and there is no apologizing for the things someone else says. No matter how much you wish you could.

"You don't have the first idea of what's happening," I hiss, and for once I don't bother hiding my ire out of respect. "I know what this looks like."

The thin veneer of civility falls away, discarded on the floor by the time we're almost nose-to-nose. "You're damn right, that's what it looks like."

"If you would for once stop to listen to someone, you'd know we had a very successful dinner with most of the city council three nights ago, and everything went beautifully. Willow has been working on—"

"You don't need to describe what Willow has been working on," he snaps. "Try all you want, son, but don't kid a kidder."

Anything I was about to say is instantly silenced when the bathroom door swings open to reveal a fully dressed, very composed Willow. We sent our clothes down to be dry cleaned earlier, and she looks fresh and poised as she strides across the room without so much as a glance my way.

"Mr. Cargill." She thrusts out a hand, looking him straight in the eye. "My name is Willow Anderson. I am the public relations professional your son hired in the wake of the video leak."

He accepts her handshake, though there's still derision dancing at the corners of his smirking mouth.

"I'm sure it was quite a shock, hearing about what's transpired over the past week or so, but rest assured, everything is firmly in control. As Sawyer just explained, the dinner meeting with the city council was nothing short of a success, and a second event scheduled to take place tomorrow afternoon should go the rest of the way toward cementing the city council's vote."

"And what miraculous event would this be?"

She lifts her chin in the face of his sarcasm. "A luncheon to celebrate a new program your family is sponsoring. The goal is to reach out to underprivileged children and provide them with free sailing lessons."

"And they'll have the opportunity to use what they've learned... when, exactly?"

"That's up to them," she fires back, unruffled except for the fresh color in her cheeks. "The point is, the Cargill family is going to be more than just a name associated with a yacht club. Much like the expansion of the club will foster a greater sense of community, so will this program. We need the public to see your family as a true contributor to this town."

"We already are," he insists, his chest puffing.

"Just the same. This is the sort of announcement that stirs up a lot of good will, and that good will takes us the rest of the way to the finish line."

I think I just witnessed a miracle. Never has anyone so effortlessly silenced Alistair Cargill. "I…" That's the best he can do while the crackling tension begins to dissipate. I wonder if she has the slightest clue what a victory she just scored.

"And in case you're wondering," she continues, folding her hands in front of her and throwing back her shoulders, "I do realize how unprofessional this incident is, and I take responsibility for it. I intend to maintain my position until the luncheon has concluded."

She what? "Willow—"

"After that," she says, raising her voice to be heard over me, "I intend to resign."

22

WILLOW

"At least we got the deposit. That's still an awful lot of money."

"Yeah, onward and upward, right?" The thing is, no matter how I fight to put on a happy face for my best friend's sake, I'm numb. Like my body's been dipped in icy water. I'm not sure how I'm functioning, honestly, considering I barely got a wink of sleep all night after taking an Uber back to the city. It didn't exactly feel right to ask for the helicopter in the wake of my resignation.

Sarah rubs my shoulder, offering an awkward half smile before biting her lip. "Are you going to be okay?"

"Define okay," I manage with a weak laugh. "Sure, I guess. With time, everything will be fine. We'll be able to expand the way we've talked about for so long, for one thing."

"You know what I mean. The business isn't what I'm concerned with."

"Isn't it?" I ask, lifting an eyebrow in the face of her support. "I mean, it's your livelihood."

"And you're my best friend."

"Listen. If I'm hurting, it's nobody's fault but my own. Truly. I walked into this with my eyes wide open."

"I know," she murmurs, leaning against the corner of my desk. I hate seeing her look so worried and want to tell her not to bother, but it would only come off the wrong way with my emotions bubbling so close to the surface. I can't take my frustration and pain out on her.

And to think, I have to go back there in a couple of hours. I can't skip the luncheon. For one thing, I told Alistair I'd be there. I'm not going to back down. I will not tuck my tail between my legs and hide.

"I'm telling you, any lingering questions about how Sawyer got to be the way he is were answered the second that man barged into the room." Just the vaguest memory makes me shudder from head to toe. I will never forget the way my stomach dropped at the sight of him. "He made me feel cheap and pitiful. The only time I ever felt that small was back at school."

"You want me to beat him up for you?"

Her sudden question paired with the way she blurted it out works its magic, and suddenly I'm laughing. She joins me, and it isn't long before we're both giggling helplessly with tears in our eyes. The thought of my gorgeous, model perfect friend throwing down against a shrewd old man is almost too funny, but strangely gratifying to imagine.

Finally, once we're both blotting our tears away with tissues, I admit, "I only resigned to take the heat off Sawyer. It's not like I wanted to. Do you think he thinks I wanted to?"

"I'm not the person to answer that question, and we both know it. Why don't you try giving him a call and asking for yourself?"

"I can't do that."

"Why in the world not?"

"You don't think I want to call him?" I pick up my phone from the desk, where I dropped it like a guilty child when she entered my office. "Do you want to know what I was doing when you barged in here? I was staring at his contact in my phone, debating on whether or not I should go through with a call."

"Why didn't you go through with it?"

"Because you walked in."

"Stop being cute. I mean it. Why haven't you called him by now?"

My mouth opens. My mouth closes. "I don't know," I finally admit. "Maybe I don't know what to say. And I'm afraid of going too far, saying the wrong thing. There's a difference between knowing he's aware of what an asshole his father is, and actually coming out and saying it."

"But this isn't about him. It's about the two of you."

"There is no two of us. He is a client. That's it." I don't sound like I mean it, probably because I don't. He's been more than a client since the beginning.

"Fair enough." She makes a big deal of checking the time before pushing off my desk. "Well, you'd better get moving if you want to make it up there in time for the luncheon."

The luncheon. I have never dreaded an event the way I'm dreading this. Knowing exactly what Alistair Cargill thinks of me, but having to smile and be polite just the same. For someone working in public relations, it seems odd that I'm so uncomfortable with the idea of faking my reaction to him. I guess it's one thing to put on a pleasant, professional aura when you aren't directly involved.

Funny how I've lectured countless clients on the finer points of behaving themselves in front of their adversaries. Now I have to follow my own advice no matter how much I don't feel like it.

I should at least call Sawyer and let him know I'm coming—then again, he hasn't called me, has he? It's probably petty of me to think about it that way, but I can't help it. The phone works both ways. If anything, he should be the one to call me and apologize for his father's rudeness. He could at least let me know he doesn't see me the way the old man immediately did.

I'll call him. I'll make the first move, be the bigger person. That's who I am, anyway. I've always known it. We can keep it professional, the way it should have been from the beginning. I can forget the thrill of his touch, the way he kisses, how right it felt to have him inside me.

I'm torturing myself, plain and simple.

The sudden buzzing from the phone makes me jump, so startled I almost drop it on the floor before pulling myself together. For one wild second I expect it to be Sawyer, like he was thinking of me the way I've been thinking about him pretty much every single minute since I left the hotel last night.

No such luck. The call is coming from Somerset Harbor according to the area code, but I don't have the number programmed in my phone. I have no idea who I'm about to speak to when I touch the green button to answer the call before raising the phone to my ear. "Hello?"

As planned, the luncheon has been set up on the back terrace between the club's dining room and the harbor beyond it. It's an absolutely superb day, weather wise; clear skies, deep blue, and the fresh breeze coming off the water is strong enough to stir the hair at the nape of my neck without teasing any strands free from the bun pinned securely in place there. All in all, we couldn't ask for anything better.

All that's left is the appearance of the club's CEO, who has yet to show his face.

The former CEO, meanwhile, has made it a point to show his face today. I guess when you're the patriarch of the Cargill family, you can invite yourself to events like this without pushback. He reminds me so much of Sawyer it's almost scary. Like looking into the future at the man his son will one day be.

Except no, not quite. Sawyer has time to pump the brakes and change course. He doesn't have to become the arrogant, dismissive man I met last night.

The man who now exchanges a look with me. When he arches an eyebrow, I lift my shoulders in a subtle gesture. I'm not sure what he wants from me. If he doesn't want things to look funny between me and his son, he shouldn't expect me to go running after Sawyer and cajole him into coming downstairs. This would all be going much more smoothly if Alistair had stayed in the Virgin Islands and kept his nose out of it.

In the meantime, I busy myself handing out the press release mere hours after Sarah gave it her approval. Normally, I would have let Sawyer pick at it, but we didn't exactly have the time. That's my fault, too. We wasted an entire day yesterday, and for what?

Nope. I'm not asking myself that question now. This isn't the time to indulge in memories that will only break my heart.

"Once Mr. Cargill joins us, he'll answer any questions you might have," I promise to more than one attendee as I move through the crowd milling around the tables.

"Alistair, I've got to hand it to you." Rob Myers' voice rings out an instant before I look up to find him shaking hands with Sawyer's father. "This girl you hired knows her business."

"Oh, that was none of my doing," Alistair is quick to clarify. To his credit, he manages to say it without a smirk, but then I think we understand each other a little better than we did before. At least, I understand him better after his phone call earlier.

"No, it was Sawyer who made the right move," he concludes, his smile widening when he catches something over my shoulder. "Speak of the devil."

Damn it. I'm sure my smile looks more like a grimace while my stomach does flips. No matter how I thought I was prepared for this, it's clear nothing could prepare me for coming face-to-face with the only man who's ever been able to convince me to forget everything I know is right, professional, and smart.

"Good afternoon, everyone." Nobody would guess at the nerves I'm sure he must be suffering from as he makes his way through the group, shaking hands, murmuring his appreciation. "I'm very sorry to have kept you waiting."

Once he reaches me, there's a subtle shift in his expression. It hurts to the point of physical pain to hold myself away from him. To pretend there's nothing between us but a professional relationship, that I didn't effectively quit my job last night. Then again, if everything goes the way it's supposed to this afternoon, he won't need me anymore, anyway.

I have to try to be happy about that. It means I did a good job.

"You're only a few minutes late," I murmur, falling in step beside him, checking my tablet. "Are you okay with the talking points?"

"I'm just fine." I can't decide if there's resentment in his clipped response, or if he's playing the part of a busy, distracted executive. There's definitely no warmth, that much is for sure, and I have to accept that. It was always going to be this way. I only fooled myself into thinking otherwise.

He reaches the small podium set up especially for today's event and flashes a winning smile while the guests settle in at their tables. Has a man ever looked better in a dark suit than Sawyer Cargill does at this particular moment? He is the living, breathing definition of success. Beauty. Fitness. All of it and more, rolled up in one exquisite package that tends to make my heart skip a beat. It takes real effort to pry my eyes away from him before anybody notices me ogling him and comes to their own conclusions.

"Good afternoon," he begins, his voice ringing with calm confidence. "First and foremost, thank you all for taking time out of your busy schedules to be here. Today marks the beginning of a new era in not only the story of the Somerset Harbor Yacht Club, but in the history of the Cargill family, as well. The initiative I'm announcing today is intended as a means of enriching the community and affirming once and for all my family's commitment to bettering the lives of not only members of our club, but of each and every resident of our community."

For the first time since his appearance, he looks down at me rather than avoiding my gaze. "In large part, this is thanks to the brilliance and patience of Willow Anderson. My girlfriend."

His girlfriend?

Somebody catch me. I think I'm going to faint.

23

SAWYER

She's good. I'll give her that.

I'm not sure what I expected her to do. I wasn't even sure I would use the word until it was already tumbling out of my mouth.

It's funny, really, how certain situations align your priorities in the blink of an eye. All it took was watching Willow leave the hotel last night, with her head held high In spite of the humiliation my father put her through, to know there's no living without this woman. I'm not going to watch her walk away again, ever.

She takes it well, showing no reaction other than a few quick blinks. Well, she didn't slap me or throw anything at me, so I'll take that as a win for now.

"As you can see in the press release Willow so helpfully handed out," I continue, lifting my own copy from the podium, "we intend to kick off a program which will allow underprivileged youths in our community to take sailing lessons for free."

It was Willow's idea to invite the board to this, and I remember why I was against the idea when Nathan lifts a finger, clearing his throat even though I haven't stepped back to allow questions just yet. "With all due respect, Mr. Cargill, and speaking as a board member, to what end will you offer these lessons? If these kids can't afford to learn to sail on their own, what good does it do to teach them a skill they more than likely won't ever make use of?"

Maybe I'm more of an idealist than I believed. I honestly couldn't imagine anyone asking such an ignorant question, at least not while in front of a couple dozen people. My gaze brushes over my father's scowling face, and that doesn't exactly leave me feeling warm and fuzzy, either.

There's a gentle tug on my sleeve, the only warning Willow gives me before practically shoving me aside. Alright, she doesn't shove, but it feels that way to be suddenly replaced at the podium. "If I might, sir, I would like to address your point. It's a point we considered while putting this plan together, and it's my personal experience which I think sold the idea."

"How so?"

"You see, what Mr. Cargill hasn't told you is, the two of us attended the same boarding school years ago. Only I was a scholarship student who would never otherwise have dreamed of sharing a classroom or a dorm with people like the Cargills and the other affluent families of those kids attending. I can't pretend there weren't times when I felt like an outsider, but at the end of the day, that experience showed me a world far bigger and richer than anything I had seen first-hand up to that point."

She pauses for effect, scanning the crowd. "My education didn't stop at history and calculus. I saw what was possible, and I became determined to work hard and earn my place at the table... so to speak. Having that school on my college applications, along with my history of academic performance, earned me a spot at the University of Pennsylvania. There I was, a girl from a single parent home where struggle was a way of life, attending an Ivy League school. Now, my business partner and I run a successful public relations firm in the heart of Manhattan and we're on the verge of expansion. I don't know that any of it would have been possible If I hadn't taken that first step."

If it weren't for the dozens of pairs of eyes staring at us, I would throw my arms around her and kiss her until she fainted for lack of oxygen. A quick look over the group shows plenty of understanding smiles, gentle nodding. Even my father manages to look impressed, watching Willow with a look of cool appraisal. It's a hell of a lot better than the disdain he treated her to last night. The fact that she's even here in the first place is a testament to her character, her strength, her everything.

"There's really not much else to say, is there?" I ask with a chuckle once the podium is mine again. "Please, feel free to approach me with any questions you might have. Considering I kept all of you waiting, it would be rude of me to keep you from your lunch a minute longer. Enjoy."

There's a soft smattering of applause before Dad rises from his seat and joins us near the railing. It's only when he grins that I'm able to breathe. "Well done," he murmurs, shaking my hand.

I can't decide whether or not it's an act for the benefit of witnesses until he turns his attention to Willow and shakes her hand as well. "I'm glad we understand each other. And as I said on the phone, I hope you can forgive my terrible behavior."

On the phone? "When did this happen?" I ask, looking back and forth between them.

Dad snickers before winking at Willow. "You don't need to know about everything," he informs me, patting my shoulder before heading over to chat with Nathan and some of the other board members. All I can do is watch, stunned.

"It looks like you're not the only one who's full of surprises today," Willow murmurs. With her back to the crowd, she narrows her eyes at me. "What was that all about? Your girlfriend? Since when?"

I'm barely able to signal for her silence before Rob Myers reaches us. "Sawyer, I thought you'd both like to know it looks like you've got the votes you need for your expansion."

Amazing, the weight a few well-chosen words can take off a man's shoulders. I have to glance down at the planks beneath my feet to confirm I'm still making contact with them instead of floating. "That is great news," I somehow manage to choke out, while Willow beams. "Thank you so much for your faith."

"When you have such an outstanding partner at your side, faith comes easily." He winks at her before turning away.

And as soon as he does, her smile evaporates. "Can I speak privately with you?" She's already walking inside by the time she finishes the question, so there's nothing to do but follow in her footsteps until we end up in what used to pass for our banquet room. Funny how small it seems now that I know the expansion plans are good to go.

She reaches the window overlooking the water before spinning on her heel, glaring at me. Even now, framed by the picturesque background while practically spitting fire, she's breathtaking. There were a few moments this morning when I was unsure whether I would see her today, making her a sight for sore eyes now. All I want is to touch her, hold her, but something tells me I'd lose a hand if I so much as attempted it.

"What the hell was that about? Just another ploy to get them to like you?"

"What?"

"Calling me your girlfriend. Did it not occur to you that's something we should have discussed before you blurted it out?"

"You honestly think I would make that up for the sake of good will?"

"What other explanation is there?"

"Did it ever occur to you I might've meant it?" While she stammers and sputters, I take the opportunity to join her by the window.

"So it wasn't an act?" she whispers, her brows drawing together.

"I can't tell if you'd rather I say yes or no."

Her mouth screws up in a scowl before she lands an ineffective shove on my shoulder. I grab her wrist before she can pull it back, then press my lips to her knuckles. "I meant it. I shouldn't have surprised you like that, but I couldn't help myself. I see what I want, and I take it. I want you."

"So you announce our relationship in public? And now, if I don't agree, everyone will know we aren't together. That is some manipulative shit."

"I promise you, that's not how I intended it. Willow, last night I had no choice but to watch you walk away. Call it a moment of clarity, but I realized then and there I don't ever want to be in that position again. I want you. Always."

Slowly, her gaze softens along with the rest of her. The creases smooth out between her brows, and her scowl turns to something gentler. “Well, let's not start making wedding plans yet. I'm not trying to rush things. We both still have our businesses and people who count on us.”

If my heart swells much more, there won’t be enough room in my chest. “Of course.”

Finally, her eyes twinkle. “But… *always* does sound good. Who would have thought the boy who made me miserable in high school and the man of my dreams would end up being the same person?”

I’ve gone entirely too long without kissing this woman, whose face I now take between my palms before touching my lips to hers. The fact that it feels like I’ve been kissing her all my life can’t be my imagination playing tricks on me.

But I do intend to kiss her for the rest of my life. No doubt about that.

24

WILLOW

It's a testament to my willpower that I'm able to keep a straight face while eyeing the hardhat my boyfriend wears and the spade he holds in one hand. "Are you ready for this?"

"I've been ready for this for weeks."

"You sure you know how to use that thing?" I tease, eyeing the spade.

"Ha, ha," he groans, rolling his eyes. "I'll have you know I can handle basic tools. I just wish I understood why we have to go through with this clown show."

"It's a ceremony, and it's just the way things are done. You break ground on a new project, you lift a spade full of dirt. Life is full of compromises."

He can complain all he wants, but I'm not fooled. He is thrilled beyond belief to be breaking ground today on the new expansion. The weeks of planning and coordinating and soothing frazzled nerves have paid off.

At a signal from the photographer, I offer a gentle nudge toward the roped-off area designated for the ceremony. "You better get a move on if we're ever going to get this party started." Because at the end of the day, that's what the dozens of people who gathered at the yacht club are here for. If they wanted to watch a spade of dirt being lifted, they could see that on the news tonight. And they will since the local news station showed up to do a story for tonight's broadcast.

In other words, everything's clicking. We're finally at the top of the mountain, and the view looks pretty damn marvelous from here.

"Wish me luck?" he asks with a twinkle in his eye.

I press a kiss against his cheek before nudging him again. "You don't need luck. You're a Cargill."

"Funny. I was about to say you're my good luck charm." As always, he needs to have the last word. The shit-eating grin he wears while approaching the designated area would have boiled my blood mere weeks ago. Now, I can only shake my head while my heart flutters. He's absolutely impossible, but I wouldn't have him any other way.

"Thank you all for coming out today." He holds the microphone in one hand, the shovel in the other. Somehow, he even manages to make a hard hat and a suit look good together. "I would be disingenuous if I said this conclusion seemed inevitable. There were some dark, difficult moments along the way—most of which were of my own doing," he adds with a self-deprecating chuckle while his father laughs knowingly from his position at Sawyer's right side.

Then he looks my way, and even though we're outside I would swear somebody took all the air away. I can't breathe. Not when he looks at me the way he is now. There is so much behind his eyes, enough to make my knees weak and my pulse race. "I couldn't have done this without Willow by my side. She's the one who did the heavy lifting throughout all of this. None of it would have been possible without the woman I love working so tirelessly on this project."

He loves me?

There he goes again, dropping something like that on me in public. He's never said that before.

And damn it, why is there still that nagging little doubt in the back of my head? His penchant for making big moments like this public triggers the pessimistic side of me, I guess.

There's a smile plastered on my face as I watch him sink the spade into the soft earth and lift a clump before tossing it aside. I'm still reeling by the time he hands off the spade and the hard hat, making a beeline for me while the crowd applauds.

He leans down, his lips brushing my ear. "I meant it," he whispers, his breath tickling my skin. "I love you."

Rather than put words to the feeling that's existed in my heart, I whisper back, "One of these days, we're going to have to talk about your penchant for making announcements like that in public."

Before either of us can say a word, we're interrupted by his brother, Brooks. "Here, you two." He hands us champagne flutes before nodding toward the club, where well-dressed guests are already beginning to wander inside for the party. "If anybody deserves to enjoy the night, it's the two of you."

"You had better enjoy yourself, too," Sawyer counters. "You're going to be a hell of a lot busier once the expansion is complete. We'll have more room than ever for all the events you love coordinating."

"You know I look forward to the opportunity." The two of them exchange a look that can only mean trouble. Something tells me he's more interested in the notion of being surrounded by bridesmaids than just about anything else.

We hang around until most of the guests are inside, with Sawyer greeting as many members as possible with me at his side. It's another twenty minutes or so before we're finally able to enter the banquet room, where soft music and candlelight weave an almost intoxicating tapestry. The gentle laughter, the sparkle of champagne flutes passing through on silver trays, all of it works together to create something as close to enchantment as I can imagine.

Or maybe that's just the thrill of knowing our hard work paid off. Maybe it's a little bit of both.

"You're born to this, you know," I muse once we step onto the dance floor and he pulls me close.

"What? Dancing with you? Because I would agree with that."

"I meant your job, but the dancing is a close second." I rest my left hand on his muscular shoulder, while his left hand engulfs my right. "Because it's more than a job to you. It's your life, it's part of you. You're charming, gracious, easy on the eyes..."

"Just easy on the eyes? What about gorgeous? Sexy?"

"Careful, or you'll make me regret complimenting you." All he does is laugh, and that sound is sweeter than any music. I'm pretty sure I love him, too. It has to be love, or else why does my heart soar when he smiles down at me?

"Well. Look who it is."

I follow the direction of Sawyer's gaze to find Brooks dancing with a pretty blonde. "Who is she?"

"That's Zoe. You remember I introduced you to Quinn, Brooks' best friend?"

"The one who runs the seafood restaurant?"

"That's the one. Zoe's his little sister. She moved to New York years ago—I think she was working for a Mompreneur the last I heard."

"That's interesting. Does she come home often?"

"This is the first time I've seen her in as long as I can remember."

It doesn't take long to size up the situation between them. "They don't look like strangers." No, in fact, if they get much closer she'll be wearing his clothes. I know what happens to a girl once a Cargill man decides to turn on the charm. She doesn't stand a chance, in other words.

"Oh. Here comes trouble." All of a sudden Sawyer releases my waist, taking me by the hand and leading me to where Brooks and Zoe tease and flirt. That's not the problem, I realize. It's Quinn, his face red, his eyes narrowed into slits as he approaches from the opposite direction. If I didn't know better, I would think he wanted to kill Brooks.

When Brooks sees us coming, he follows the direction of his brother's troubled gaze to find Quinn storming his way. We're close enough to them that I hear him say, "It looks like I'm keeping you from socializing." Suddenly he takes his hands off Zoe's slim waist like she'd burned him.

I feel bad for her obvious confusion, but that quickly evaporates once she spots her brother. The fact that she doesn't look the slightest bit surprised tells a story of its own.

"Hey, Quinn," Sawyer offers with a tight grin. "Glad you could take a little time away from the restaurant to join us tonight."

Quinn manages the briefest nod before turning his attention back to Brooks. “What do you think you're doing?”

“What are you talking about?” Brooks asks while Zoe ducks into the crowd, weaving her way through before vanishing.

“You know what I'm talking about. It was nice of Zoe to come out to celebrate tonight, but I didn't think it would mean you'd be feeling her up on the dance floor.”

“Quinn, take it easy.” I have to give Sawyer credit. He's learned how to conceal what he's thinking in public. No way is he anything less than irritated, but he’s the picture of charming hospitality.

Quinn ignores him, too busy glaring at Brooks. “Maybe you can be a man whore with some other guy's sister, but this is my sister we’re talking about.”

Brooks only holds up his hands, chuckling. “Calm down. We were just catching up since it's been a while since we've seen each other.”

Quinn merely scoffs. “That's not what it looked like to me.” Frankly, that's not what it looked like to me, either. But I know better than to insert my opinion.

"Maybe you should get all the facts together before you try to attack your best friend at a party, right?" Brooks slings an arm around his shoulders. "Come on. Let's get a drink." All we can do is watch them walk away together. It's clear from the tension running through Quinn's body that he's not going to let it go so easily.

"I don't know how you guys do it," I murmur, watching them walk away.

"How we do what?"

"Keeping your cool in a situation like that. He diffused it so well."

Sawyer snickers, pulling me close again. "He's had plenty of experience explaining himself to big brothers."

"You guys sure do get around, don't you?" I pull my head back to look up at him, scowling. "I hope you've gotten that out of your system."

The arm around my waist tightens, and there is nothing about the way he looks at me that leaves any room for doubt. "Trust me, Willow Anderson. Those days are behind me. As far as I'm concerned, you are the only woman who exists."

I think I can live with that.

I know I can.

25

SAWYER

"Already, we have people calling to reserve dates six, eight, ten months from now." Brooks raises his glass to me from his seat on the other side of my desk. "I have to admit, you pulled it off."

After all this work, doubt, and anxiety, a nice glass of Scotch goes down smoother than ever. "What can I say? I'm just that good."

"You mean you just so happened to call somebody who is just that good."

"Silly me, thinking my little brother would grant me a small bit of leeway for once."

"Not a chance."

Setting my glass aside, I eye him carefully. Aside from our present banter, he's been strangely quiet and humorless since the groundbreaking a few days ago. "I've been meaning to ask you. How are things between you and Quinn? Has he finally calmed down?"

He winces before shrugging. "I'm honestly not sure. He says everything's fine, but something tells me it's only because Zoe's out of town again. Oh, well. It's for the best." He looks genuinely crestfallen, and I can't help but wonder if for once he wishes he didn't play the field so aggressively.

"I'm sorry to hear that. You two looked like you were having a good time, too."

He bolts back the rest of his drink before shrugging. "Anyway, it's in the past. I'd better get downstairs—there's a newly engaged couple coming in to take a tour before they schedule their reception. I'll hand it to that girlfriend of yours."

"You'll hand what to me?"

I can't stifle a chuckle when he turns in the chair to find Willow watching from the doorway. In her tailored suit and stilettoes, she's the picture of a professional. She's also the sexiest, most irresistible thing I've ever seen.

Brooks stammers before clearing his throat. "Oh. I was about to compliment you on the work you've done to keep the club in the news. I can't keep up with all the phone calls."

"Mm-hmm." When he makes a pained noise, she giggles and waves a hand. "Come on. I'm messing with you. There are another four news spots scheduled for the coming weeks to keep the public abreast of the new construction, too. So get ready for more calls."

"She's good," he tells me with a sigh as he stands. "And she's making me earn my salary."

"Speaking of which…" I lower my brow before jerking my chin toward the door. *Get out of here and give me a minute alone with my girl.* He gets the message and, with a slight salute, saunters out of the office before closing the door behind him.

"Alone at last." I flash a wolfish grin before standing, extending my arms. "Come here."

"Not until I get your eyes on this agreement for the interview I scheduled with the Times." She holds up a folder, her brow lifting in expectation.

"I'd rather get my eyes on something else…" I'm a hair's breadth from touching her when she darts away, shaking her head.

"Come on, now," she chides, though there's soft laughter in her voice. "I want to get this finished before I head back."

Just like that, my excitement falters. The thought of her returning to Manhattan is about as effective a boner killer as anything I can think of. "Who says you have to go back?" I ask as we face each other from opposite ends of the desk.

"Let's see." She holds up one finger. "My landlord." A second. "My plants, which Sarah has been tending while I've been here."

"I'll take care of your lease, and you can bring your plants here."

She barks out a disbelieving laugh, her gaze never drifting from my face. I can see the wheels turning in that methodical brain of hers. "You aren't serious."

"Who says?" I sweep an arm toward the window. "This could be your view from now on—well, you could have an office of your own here at the club."

"And why would I have an office here?"

"Doesn't it make sense for the new Cargill PR manager to have an office here at the club?"

Her eyelids flutter. "You aren't serious." This time, it's a whisper.

"Why do you keep saying that? Of course, I'm serious. I want you here."

She lowers the folder to the desk, then props her palms on the surface. "I have a business of my own."

"Which could continue running with you as a consultant."

"Don't make decisions for me."

The firmness in the way she says it brings me up short. "You're right. But it's something worth considering."

"I love my work," she insists. "And I doubt there'd be enough here to keep me busy on a full-time basis."

"Who knows?" I probably shouldn't, but I can't help lifting a shoulder. "I could screw up again and make a lot more work for you."

"Please," she warns. "This is a big deal. I need you to understand how important it is for me to make my own choices."

"Fair enough. But you can't blame a guy for trying."

"Besides." She straightens up, then folds her arms. "I don't have to take crappy jobs anymore. My last client paid too much, so I can afford to be choosy."

"Very cute."

"Okay, okay." She moves slowly, creeping toward me while fighting back a grin. "I guess, if I had to, I could work remotely—whether I'm here or at the office in New York. I could handle both."

A spark of hope flares to lift in my chest. Incredible, the way my life hinges on this woman. Her presence, her smell, her touch. "You think so?"

"It helps that I know a guy who happens to own a helicopter I can take back and forth whenever I want to." Finally, she drops the act, laughing as she steps into the circle of my arms. This is where she belongs, close to me, standing on tiptoe for a kiss that only leads to another kiss, then another.

"Okay," she agrees while I skim her jaw with my lips. "I accept, so long as you can accept my having other clients."

"So long as none of those clients are men. I might have to accidentally-on-purpose cause another scandal to keep all of your attention for myself."

"You would have to go and say something like that. I swear, if you do anything of the sort—"

"You know I'm only kidding," I insist while she tries to squirm her way out of my embrace.

"I don't know any such thing, Sawyer Cargill."

"What? Your opinion of me is that low?"

She pauses for a beat before frowning. "No comment."

"I love you," I finally laugh, pulling her close again. "I do. I love your refusal to take shit from me. I love how you always think you're right."

"I am always right," she grumbles. "Well, almost always."

"When were you wrong?"

She reaches up to run a hand over my cheek. "When I assumed you hadn't changed. When I was sure I knew the real you. And now that I think about it, there's something left unspoken between us."

I have to brace myself before asking, "What's that?"

"I love you, too."

It's inevitable, the way we're drawn together. She tips her head back and I practically devour her plump, sweet mouth. The only woman I'll ever kiss again. The only woman I'll ever want to kiss again.

Her fingers tangle in my hair before the hunger that naturally springs to life between us leaves us both panting, and she offers no resistance before I back her against the desk and part her legs with one of mine.

"We should find someplace a little more discreet," she whispers before whimpering at the touch of my fingers against her inner thigh. "What happens if somebody walks in?"

"Oh, no," I whisper, creeping higher until the enticing heat coming from her mound makes me groan in helpless desire. "That would be a PR nightmare. You'd have to work overtime to clean up a mess that big."

"Keep it up with the jokes," she warns before moaning softly, bearing down on my hand and rocking her hips. "We'll see how much further this goes."

When our eyes meet and she lifts an eyebrow in a silent challenge, I know one thing for sure: this maddening woman was made for me.

And I could happily spend the rest of my life being put in my place… so long as she's the one doing it.

"Have I mentioned the dressing room behind that wall?" I ask, tipping my head in the direction of the hidden door. "And the bed inside?"

Her wicked grin is fuel poured over the fire of my endless need for her. "See? I knew we could come to a compromise."

"What can I say?" I take her hand, leading the way. "I'm highly motivated."

THANK you for reading Hate Mate. We hope you enjoyed Willow and Sawyer's story. Can't get enough and want an extra steamy scene? **Grab your FREE Hate Mate Bonus Chapter now!**

Want more from the Cargills? Can't wait to find out what happens to Sawyer's brother, Brooks, and Zoe? **1-Click Best Laid Plans Now!**

Brooks Cargill can have any woman in the world except for one: his best friend's sister.

I'm an a-hole, a manwhore and a workaholic and everything else that everyone

calls me. The only loyalty I have is to my brothers and my best friend, Quinn. That's what makes this so hard. The only woman I really want and can't ever pursue is Quinn's little sister.

For years, I've done my best to put Zoe out of my mind, but then Quinn puts me in charge of coordinating the plans to his upcoming wedding at my family's Somerset Harbor Yacht Club.

Now, I can't avoid Zoe any longer. And damn, does she look good. As we work together to create the perfect wedding, I can't help but want her more and more.

One night, after a few too many drinks, Zoe and I give in to our desires and have a wild night of passion. We agree to keep it a secret, knowing that Quinn would lose his mind if he found out.

But I can't stop thinking about her, and it seems like she can't stop thinking about me either.

What if this secret comes out?

What if I put everything on the line and lose it all?

✅ Brother's best friend romance

✅ Sunny vs grumpy

✅ Second chance

✅ Billionaire romance

✅ Small exclusive wealthy town romance

Best Laid Plans is a scorching hot brother's best friend romance, features a strong heroine and a billionaire she'd love to hate.

Throw in some unforgettable nights of passion, battles of wills and you have the perfect summer romance.

Grab your copy of Best Laid Plans now!

WANT TO BE THE FIRST TO KNOW ABOUT MY UPCOMING SALES, NEW RELEASES AND EXCLUSIVE GIVEAWAYS?

Sign up for my newsletter and get a FREE book: https://dl.bookfunnel.com/gp3o8yvmxd

Join my Facebook Group: https://www.facebook.com/groups/276340079439433/

Bonus Points: Follow me on BookBub and Goodreads!

ALSO BY CHARLOTTE BYRD

All books are available at ALL major retailers! If you can't find it, please email me at charlotte@charlotte-byrd.com

Somerset Harbor

Hate Mate (Cargill Brothers 1)

Best Laid Plans (Cargill Brothers 2)

Picture Perfect (Cargill Brothers 3)

Always Never (Cargill Brothers 4)

Tell me Series

Tell Me to Stop

Tell Me to Go

Tell Me to Stay

Tell Me to Run

Tell Me to Fight

Tell Me to Lie

Tell Me to Stop Box Set Books 1-6

Black Series

Black Edge

Black Rules

Black Bounds

Black Contract

Black Limit

Black Edge Box Set Books 1-5

Dark Intentions Series

Dark Intentions

Dark Redemption

Dark Sins

Dark Temptations

Dark Inheritance

Dark Intentions Box Set Books 1-5

Tangled Series

Tangled up in Ice

Tangled up in Pain

Tangled up in Lace

Tangled up in Hate

Tangled up in Love

Tangled up in Ice Box Set Books 1-5

The Perfect Stranger Series

The Perfect Stranger

The Perfect Cover

The Perfect Lie

The Perfect Life

The Perfect Getaway

The Perfect Stranger Box Set Books 1-5

Wedlocked Trilogy

Dangerous Engagement

Lethal Wedding

Fatal Wedding

Dangerous Engagement Box Set Books 1-3

Lavish Trilogy

Lavish Lies

Lavish Betrayal

Lavish Obsession

Lavish Lies Box Set Books 1-3

All the Lies Series

All the Lies

All the Secrets

All the Doubts

All the Lies Box Set Books 1-3

Not into you Duet

Not into you

Still not into you

Standalone Novels

Dressing Mr. Dalton

Debt

Offer

Unknown

ABOUT CHARLOTTE BYRD

Charlotte Byrd is the bestselling author of romantic suspense novels. She has sold over 1.5 Million books and has been translated into five languages.

She lives near Palm Springs, California with her husband, son, a toy Australian Shepherd and a Ragdoll cat. Charlotte is addicted to books and Netflix and she loves hot weather and crystal blue water.

Write her here:

charlotte@charlotte-byrd.com

Check out her books here:

www.charlotte-byrd.com

Connect with her here:

www.tiktok.com/charlottebyrdbooks

www.facebook.com/charlottebyrdbooks

www.instagram.com/charlottebyrdbooks

Sign up for my newsletter: https://www.subscribepage.com/byrdVIPList

Join my Facebook Group: https://www.facebook.com/groups/276340079439433/

Bonus Points: Follow me on BookBub and Goodreads!

amazon.com/Charlotte-Byrd/e/B013MN45Q6

facebook.com/charlottebyrdbooks

tiktok.com/charlottebyrdbooks

bookbub.com/profile/charlotte-byrd

instagram.com/charlottebyrdbooks

twitter.com/byrdauthor